"It's really kind of you to help, Mr. Sullivan," Alexis replied,

"but I don't want to put you out. You have your shop to get back to and Cliff to take care of. Why don't I just—"

"Miss Richmond—" J.D. held the truck door wide and held out a helping hand her way "—we'll have you home in no time."

"Oh...um...thank you." J.D. slipped his hand under her elbow as she stepped up to reach the truck floor. For half an instant, she felt his warm breath on her cheek. Then she was up and seated on the black leather seat next to Cliff. "I do appreciate it," she said, turning just as his eyes lifted from her legs. His mouth softened as his gaze skittered away. She tugged her skirt back to her knees, feeling her cheeks flush.

She hadn't blushed in years.

Books by Ruth Scofield

Love Inspired

In God's Own Time #29
The Perfect Groom #65
Whispers of the Heart #89
Wonders of the Heart #124
Loving Thy Neighbor #145
Take My Hand #219

RUTH SCOFIELD

became serious about writing after she'd raised her children. Until then, she'd concentrated her life on being a June Cleaver-type wife and mother, spent years as a Bible student and teacher for teens and young adults and led a weekly women's prayer group. When she'd made a final wedding dress and her last child had left the nest, she declared to one and all that it was her turn to activate a dream. Thankfully, her husband applauded her decision.

Ruth's first book was published in 1993 just a month after her return to her native Missouri after years in the East. She often sets her novels in Missouri, where there are lakes and hills aplenty, and as many stories and history as people. She eagerly expects to write two dozen more novels.

TAKE MY HAND

RUTH SCOFIELD

Love Inspired

Published by Steeple Hill Books™

STEEPLE HILL BOOKS

Steeple
Hill®

ISBN 0-373-87226-7

TAKE MY HAND

Visit us at www.steeplehill.com

Printed in U.S.A.

And now these three remain: faith, hope, and love.
But the greatest of these is love.
—*I Corinthians* 13:13

I wish to thank Karen Williamson, my daughter
and teacher of students with Behavior Disorder,
for her help in the understanding
of educational terminology.

Chapter One

Alexis Richmond looked up as a man paused in her open classroom door. He stood tall and knee-locked, his thighs molded inside his denims as though holding his own against a gale wind. His lightning glance showed dark brown eyes full of vexation, framed in tired lines.

She continued to stack papers and waited.

The father of her new student, she assumed. The Lake Trails Elementary School office had called only an hour ago to let her know her class would now number twelve. Twelve was a large group for a special-needs class. Alexis taught students classified as having a behavior disorder—often among other disabilities. Thank God for the help of Kathy, her para-professional.

The stranger's gaze took her in with a quick skim before his mouth tightened with sheer determination. He glanced behind him. "*Come on,* Cliff."

The boy eased around the corner into view. Alexis knew he was nine years old from her brief glance at the sketchy notes sent down from the office. He wore rumpled brown shorts and a T-shirt ripped at the shoulder. His knees and elbows, sporting a couple of scabs, appeared as sharp points on his skinny limbs. He looked clean, at least.

"Get in here" came through the father's gritted teeth. His large, work-worn hand clamped the boy's thin shoulder as though preventing a dash for freedom.

Now this was a great start.... Coming to a new school was *not* a happy event for this pair.

The man's jaw showed evidence of a sketchy shave, and he didn't look a whole lot neater than his son. Both could do with a good haircut. However, the boy's face looked scrubbed to a shine, and she caught the fragrance of a familiar soap.

Casual dress didn't bother her, as long as a student was clean and modest. She preferred wearing simple things herself, and today had chosen a sleeveless, flowered cotton dress that skimmed her body in loose comfort. She liked the fact that the blue print matched her eyes. She'd felt like celebrating spring this morning.

She was thankful this pair had arrived while her other students were in Music. She had about twenty minutes of quiet time before the kids returned. She usually needed the break; teaching special-needs students demanded patience and one hundred percent teacher focus. But at least now she had a few moments to give this new child her undivided attention. And the dad. They both looked a little lost, she thought.

She let out her breath. Time to take charge, she guessed. She moved out from behind the desk. "Hello. I'm Miss Richmond. And you are…?"

Far back in his dark eyes, a spark of startled awareness flickered a moment before he answered. It elicited a quick, surprised reaction in her middle. As though they had met before, somewhere. Sometime. Yet Alexis knew they hadn't.

Assuming her professional armor, she ignored the feeling.

"J.D., ma'am. J. D. Sullivan." He handed her a large brown envelope, fat with what she suspected were the child's school records. "This is my son, Clifford."

"Hi, Clifford." Alexis looked directly at the boy. "I'm glad to meet you."

The child didn't answer, but defiance gleamed from his dark brown eyes before his gaze darted to the bank of windows.

J.D. frowned. "Answer the lady, boy."

Cliff remained silent a moment, then, when his dad squeezed his shoulder, he mumbled, "'Lo." But the boy didn't return his gaze to hers.

The child's behavior was in keeping with why he'd been placed in her class. Complicating the problem, the child had just lost his mother, and Missouri was half a continent away from where he'd lived in California. All this was new to the child.

Helping Cliff, with only a few weeks left in the school year, surely presented a challenge.

Alexis sat against the edge of her desk; it brought her face closer to the child's. She softened her tone. "I know it's hard, coming into a new classroom so late in the year. But you'll make friends here, and we'll find out how to help each other. Okay?"

At the boy's continued silence, J.D. glanced at her, a hint of desperation there. Since she knew the pitfalls of getting personally caught up in the parents' plights, Alexis tried to firm her heart against that soulful gaze. But a trace of compassion seeped through.

"Never mind for the moment. Clifford, why don't you take this desk here—" she tapped the desk closest to hers "—and then go look at our aquarium back there in the corner until the other students are back from Music."

"I'm not Clifford." He thrust his chin out. "I'm Cliff."

"All right. Cliff. We have a turtle in our tank as well as fish. See if he's out on the island."

The boy impatiently shook off his dad's hand and headed toward the back corner.

"That's it, then." Relief seemed to ease some of J.D.'s tension as he half turned toward the door. "I'll pick him up at the end of the day."

"Hold on, Mr. Sullivan. We have a few things to discuss."

"Uh…like what?" A tinge of alarm edged his voice as he swung back.

"Like Cliff's needs. His school record. His meds."

"It's all there, isn't it? In that file from California?" J.D. flashed a tired, half-belligerent glance at the folder in her hand.

"I hope so, but I haven't had a chance to read it, have I?"

"I can't tell you anything more than that file can," he said, as impatient as his son. He glanced at his watch. "We got in to Doc Hanes's office this morning, so Cliff's all set now with those pills he's taking. What else is there?"

"Well, we have to set up an IEP meeting."

"A what?"

"Individualized Education Plan."

"Oh. Yeah. Well…do whatever you have to. I have to go now. I'm late getting my shop open."

Alexis tried to hide her annoyance. Most of the parents she dealt with were eager to do what was best for their child, but she ran into an occasional careless one. Like now.

From the fish tank came a drumming sound. "Cliff, don't do that!" his father called. Cliff didn't acknowledge the command to stop.

"Cliff!"

His back to them, the boy moved on to pull a book from a shelf, then flip it repeatedly with a *slap-slap* noise.

"Sorry." J.D. shoved his hands into his jeans pockets. A tired sigh escaped him with his apology.

Alexis nodded, then said, "We should do this within a week or two, Mr. Sullivan."

"It's spring, Miss Richmond. My busy time. Haven't much time for extras."

Alexis thought J.D. was about ready to bolt. She took a step forward and spoke quickly. "An IEP is a required document for any student with a disability, Mr. Sullivan. The law requires a team meeting among parents, teacher, school nurse and principal. It can't wait."

"Me? I have to be there?" Caught in surprise, his glance told her he felt totally helpless. His already dark eyes deepened to melting chocolate. Her heart gave a little kick, swimming against an unwelcome tide. *Oh, no…*

She'd run afoul of these natural charmers before, to her own sorrow. A man like this one used it without half trying, and she'd been a sucker once too often. Why couldn't she simply demand the man's help, and then forget it? He was the parent, after all. She was merely the teacher.

A tumble of books hit the cement floor.

J.D. raised his voice. "Cliff!"

"I didn't do it," the boy instantly whined. "They just fell."

"Stop getting into what you shouldn't," his father commanded. "How many times do I have to tell you that?"

Alexis calmly walked over to help pick up the books. "You may read this one while you wait, Cliff," she said, handing one to the boy. "Take your seat now. The other boys and girls will be back any moment."

Sulking, the child slumped into the seat indicated, but immediately began kicking the leg.

Well-practiced, Alexis ignored the continued noise. Time enough to work with Cliff when his emotions had settled down and he became comfortable in the classroom.

Walking back to the front of the room, she noticed J.D. had edged toward the door. "The boy is building for a good walloping before long," he muttered, running his hand through his hair. "If he doesn't straighten up soon."

Maybe J.D. wasn't so charming after all, Alexis thought. The thought of "walloping" any child put her back up. But he was a father on the edge. A parent who needed help. "I don't think a spanking would solve anything...."

He rubbed a spot between his eyes with his thumb. "Kept me up and down three nights running since he came. My ex spoiled him rotten...."

That explained some of the irritation.

"Both of you must be worn out," she said, letting her sympathy show. "It does take time to adjust to a new environment, Mr. Sullivan. I'm sure Cliff's behavior will improve once we get him settled and he understands where his boundaries are. Now about the IEP..."

"Uh-huh. Um...what is it again?"

"An Individualized Education Plan for Cliff. It sets out the goals for a child for one full calendar year. His meds intake should have a firm routine as a part of that. I'll call you after I've looked over the papers, to set up the meeting.''

"The school year is winding down, isn't it? Don't see what good it would do this late.''

"More than you can imagine, Mr. Sullivan. At least we'll have a handle on Cliff's problems for next year, as well. We need to be in agreement here, with all parties involved in full understanding of what's best for Cliff. What we're trying to accomplish for your son.''

"Yeah, okay. Well, you're the teacher,'' he said with an air of finality. "Anything you say, I'll do it.''

With that, J. D. Sullivan nearly raced from the room.

"A paddle would do more good, if you ask me,'' J.D. muttered all the way out to his truck. "Even just the threat. Brat!''

He turned the ignition key of his '79 truck, put the shift into gear and barely refrained from roaring out of the school parking lot. Here it was noon, and there was no one minding his shop.

He continued to talk to himself. "Melanie did a good job at spoiling the kid. Only one way to fix that.''

Yet J.D. wasn't ready to actually carry out his threat. He'd never laid a hand on Cliff in anger—nor on Melanie, in spite of their volatile marriage. But Cliff was only four when Melanie took him from Missouri to California, and now... J.D. simply didn't know what to do with the son now in his keeping. He'd missed the past five years of fathering.

It was all well and good for smooth-as-silk Miss Richmond to talk. With that fancy education the principal had told him about, Miss Richmond could spout with ease all that stuff that modern teachers knew about how a misbehaving child should be taught. But that wouldn't help him at home. How was he supposed to cope when Cliff hated him? When they didn't know each other? When the boy *whined* constantly?

In the alley off Sunny Creek's main street, he pulled into his spot behind the shop and sat a moment. He leaned his head against his fist, his elbow supported on the steering wheel. He let his breath whoosh from his lungs. He was already tired, and the day was only half over.

How much trouble was he in? He and his son?

What was he going to do?

Oh, Lord, I need Your help.… I feel like a dunce! I'm in over my head here and I don't know how to handle my own son. Can You tell me what to do?

It had been years since he'd addressed his creator— since he was a boy. He'd neglected that aspect of his life with little guilt, finding a morning out on the lake fishing or simply sleeping late on Sundays more to his liking. Maybe the Lord wouldn't hear him anymore.

He suddenly wished he kept a Bible at the shop. Perhaps some scripture might tell him something— give him some hope. The Bible is what his mom had turned to when she felt troubled. He had a Bible at home. Somewhere. But he wouldn't even know where to look for it. Or what scripture to read.

He no longer was acquainted with any pastor in town, either. He'd feel a fool to go to one for help now, when he was desperate. Yet helping was something ministers did, wasn't it?

That was something else he'd have to look into, he supposed. A church to attend. The one he'd known as a child, perhaps. Cliff would need friends.

Well, he didn't have time to think more about it now. He'd turned off his cell phone to concentrate on getting Cliff enrolled in school. No telling how many calls he'd have waiting for him on his answering machine. Though he never ignored them, customers grew impatient when they couldn't reach him easily.

As he unlocked the rear door and flicked on lights, his mood lightened a tad. This was his refuge, his territory. This was what he did well. Small-engine parts and repair. His customers knew he was the best in Missouri at small-engine repair. His reputation was known all over the lakes. He sold boat parts and limited equipment on the side, as well.

At least Cliff was safely at school with that pretty teacher. He could relax, knowing the kid wasn't tearing up his house while he wasn't looking. At least Cliff was out of trouble. And looking at Miss Richmond all day would be no hardship. None at all, with that honey-colored hair and those cool blue-green eyes. Her delicate features positively invited masculine attention, he mused. He'd never been so lucky when he was in school.

He'd almost lost his cool when he first saw her—shucks, he had, J.D. admitted. She'd looked good enough to tuck into his pocket any day.

He wondered where she was from. He hadn't seen her around town before, and the town wasn't all that big in the winter off-season. Sunny Creek sat at the northern edge of Truman Lake, an old town now three times the size of what it was when he was a boy. She must be one of the new people.

The phone rang, and he grabbed it on the third ring. ''Sullivan's Repair,'' he answered, yanking his thoughts back from a womanly figure whose shapely calves peeking from a flowered hem had intrigued him.

It was just as well. No way would a woman like Miss Richmond look twice at a man like him. She'd go for one of those summertime intellectuals or a smart-mouth from the school board.

But you couldn't shoot a man for merely looking. At least he'd see her again at the end of the school day.

Chapter Two

Two mornings later, Alexis shook her head, an unspoken regret rattling around her thoughts. She didn't like having to call Mr. Sullivan so soon, but she had no choice. Cliff had caused a disruption. She'd expected such, but it had come more quickly than she'd anticipated.

"Kathy, can you keep an eye on things for five minutes?" Alexis treasured her para, the assistant teacher assigned to her class. Kathy, an attractive woman of middle years, had the patience of a saint. It also helped that her own child, now grown, had been a special-needs student. "I think I'll make this call from the office, if you don't mind."

"Sure, Miss Richmond. Um, I have a better idea. We'll take a trip to the library."

"Bless you," Alexis said, flashing Kathy a smile of gratitude.

Alexis waited until the students filed out, then

closed the classroom door and pulled out her cell phone. Running her finger down the list of phone numbers, she found the one she sought and punched in J.D.'s shop number. She waited tentatively. After their first meeting, she wasn't quite sure of the reception she'd get from the sexy Mr. Sullivan.

Now, why in the world had she thought of him with that tag? Sexy? She didn't usually pigeonhole people with mere skin-deep descriptions.

Yet she couldn't deny the label.

"Sullivan's Repair."

"Mr. Sullivan?" She jerked her thoughts back to the task at hand, activating her teacher's voice. "This is Alexis Richmond. We need to see you as soon as possible. Can you come in this afternoon, right after the close of the school day?"

"Middle of the afternoon? Can't do it."

"Then, how about now, Mr. Sullivan? Immediately."

"Why? What's the rush?"

"Cliff's behavior." Calling on years of practice, she kept her tone nonjudgmental. "We need to discuss discipline."

"What's he done?"

"He hit another student. Hard. We cannot tolerate improper aggression of any degree, Mr. Sullivan. If you want your child to remain in public school, we must reach an understanding on how he is to be disciplined. There is a possibility that he could be facing an out-of-school suspension."

A short silence followed, then he said, "Got into a fight, did he?"

"Not exactly." In her opinion, a fight included participation from more than one person. Tyler, the other boy, hadn't done much to defend himself. "Cliff overreacted to a...verbal disagreement."

"Is that all? Can't you just shake him or stand him in the corner?"

Is that all the man could think of? To physically punish the boy? Pursing her lips, she mentally counted to ten.

"His behavior management will be much more effective if we work as a team, Mr. Sullivan." She put an effort into firming her tone. "Cliff needs to know we are in agreement, and I don't really think he needs..."

Alexis bit her tongue. She wanted to say the child needed love and hugs along with firm limitations. He needed years of parental companionship to teach him emotional balance and self-confidence. Plus a firsthand example of appropriate control of angry emotions. She suspected the child had missed out on all that.

According to the sketchy report she'd read, perhaps the father had, too.

Alexis changed her tactic. "Have you read your son's paperwork, Mr. Sullivan?"

"Haven't had time."

Vexation flooded her thoughts, and she prayed for self-control. She brushed her hair behind her ear and shifted in her chair. How could a father be so uninterested? So what that he hadn't been a part of his son's life for years. He was the sole parent now!

But it wouldn't do to show less command of herself than she expected of her students, and this wasn't the first time she'd run into a difficult parent. The kind of problems her students exhibited often extended to include a misguided parent, but she was beginning to understand that this set of problems covered J.D. and Cliff in a different way.

So she spoke mildly. "I do hope you'll take the time within the next day or so, Mr. Sullivan. Before we hold our IEP meeting."

The next moment of silence seemed full of unspoken sentiments. Had he caught her irritation in spite of her best efforts?

"I'll get to it," he replied. "Meanwhile, Cliff can, um, just do without supper."

"That's not really the way I'd choose to help Cliff face his offense...."

Another pause. "All right. What do you want to do?"

The door swung wide, and her students trailed in, Kathy in the rear. Kathy raised her brow, a silent question conveyed. Alexis nodded, and signaled her to get the kids seated.

"I'll give Cliff an after-school detention for now," Alexis quickly said into the phone. "You can pick him up at four-thirty. Perhaps we can arrange for a meeting then?"

"Guess I can't avoid it. Okay, I'll be there."

"Fine. I'll expect you."

Breathing a sigh of thankfulness, Alexis glanced at her watch. There was just enough left of the school day to tackle a short math lesson.

J.D. surprised her by arriving a few minutes early. Almost silently. She glanced up, and he was there, staring at her with a soft gaze.

Cliff and two other students sat in her room. She'd taken after-school duty, trading another teacher for her time. Kathy had offered to stay, too, but she had put in a lot of overtime throughout the winter, so Alexis had declined.

Cliff sat at his desk, refusing to look at her. For the past two hours he hadn't looked at anyone. He'd sullenly refused to apologize to Tyler, insisting Tyler deserved his wrath. Tyler had laughed and made fun when Cliff missed hitting the ball in the softball game.

J.D. advanced into the room. "Okay, I'm here, Miss Richmond. Now what?"

"Why don't you be seated, Mr. Sullivan, until I can dismiss the other students." She briefly wondered what the "J.D." stood for—she much preferred using complete names rather than initials. "Here, take this chair."

It didn't matter. He was "Mr. Sullivan" to her.

She went about closing out the day, knowing he watched everything she did. Grown men were a rarity in her classroom. From the corner of her eye, she noted J.D.'s long legs, clad in well-washed blue jeans, as he thrust them out in front of him and crossed his ankles. Her pulse quickened.

In her specialty, parent-teacher talks were often filled with tension, but not usually this kind: male to female.

What was wrong with her? She'd just broken off a two-year relationship that had been going nowhere, and she wanted time to recover from residual feelings. She was determined to give herself at least six months to a year before dating again. Heaven knows, a crush on a student's father was certainly one thing she didn't need right now. Or anytime, for that matter. Especially a careless lump who didn't seem to have any natural instincts as a father.

Then she caught his gaze. The way he looked at her indicated he certainly didn't lack other natural instincts. He exhibited very basic ones without any problem.

This would never do. She must be having a rebound reaction....

Mentally shaking herself, Alexis stilled her riotous thoughts. She was still the teacher and she had a job to do. Turning a competent face to J.D., she murmured, "All right, now..."

They talked with Cliff for fifteen minutes as Alexis explained her reasons for insisting the boy apologize to the child he'd whacked. "You need to own up to your actions, Cliff. That's a part of growing up, you see. Learning to handle your anger correctly is tough, but I'm sure you can do it."

J.D. listened as attentively as his son, but he surprised her further when he backed her up.

"If Miss Richmond says you have to apologize,

then you have to. First thing Monday morning. Understand?"

Cliff started to debate the issue, but then, catching the stern look on his father's face, he lost some of his belligerence. "Yeah, I guess."

"Good," Alexis said. This session had gone better than she had thought it might. "I'm sure things will improve for you soon."

She excused Cliff. The child shot from his seat to glue himself to the windows.

Alexis turned to the father. "This is a positive step. It's very difficult for a child to change schools so late in the year, and adjustments are especially hard for our special students. Now let's find a time when all the professionals involved in Cliff's welfare can meet with you, Mr. Sullivan."

They set a time for early the following week. That gave J.D. time to read his son's papers, and, hopefully, think about Cliff's needs. Alexis rose and offered her hand to signal the meeting's close.

"Thank you for coming in so promptly. I'm sure Cliff will settle in soon."

"Hope so." J.D. enveloped her small hand in his and shook it twice. His touch teased her senses.

She blinked and pulled her hand away. She pressed her lips together in tight denial. Dropping her lashes, she said, "'Bye, Cliff. See you tomorrow."

Cliff dashed from the room without replying. J.D. gave her a curt nod, then turned to follow his son.

Alexis let out a long sigh, then gathered her briefcase and purse. She was eager to get home. She planned to pick up a carryout meal to drop by the home of Mrs. Nelson, a woman who attended the same church as she. The old dear had been house-bound a lot this past winter, and her daughter had recently moved. Alexis felt a heart tug to give the woman some needed company.

After that, she had a pile of papers to slog through. Plus some lesson plans to form. It would be enough to keep her from thinking too much about the sad state her personal life was in. She'd been on her way to planning a wedding when she discovered that life with Ron would never work. Ron was more interested in his ambitions than her. She'd broken off the engagement during spring break.

Alexis didn't really regret her decision. She only regretted spending too much time on a man not right for her. In the end, she'd parted from Ron without a backward glance. But at thirty, she surely did wonder what God had in store for her now.

Yes, Lord. What now? She wanted a husband of her own to grown old with, a man and children to cherish. Yet she knew...the Lord hadn't failed her. *She* was the one who kept falling for the wrong kind of guy.

Lord, am I destined to only teach children that are not my own? she couldn't help asking. *What more can I do? Will I never find an intelligent, Godly man with whom I can spend a lifetime?*

Outside, she breathed deeply in the spring air. Only two months or so left of the school year. As much as she valued and thrived on teaching, she looked for-ward to the close of the long semester. She really needed this summer's break. It was the first one in five years that she had free—she was neither teaching summer school nor attending a class.

Most of the school emptied out five minutes after the last bell rang. The spring weather coaxed everyone to enjoy the outdoors. As usual, she seemed to be one of the dawdlers. Only three cars, including her own, remained in the parking lot.

She tossed her things into the passenger seat and slid behind the wheel.

Only it wouldn't start. The motor made an irritating grinding sound, but wouldn't catch. She tried again with the same results. Then she got out of the car.

This topped her day. It really did. She felt like kicking tires or something, like one of her students might. If that would help—which it wouldn't. Her hands on her hips, she merely stared at the vehicle. Now what?

"Trouble, Miss Richmond?" A deep voice startled her.

She glanced over her shoulder. J.D. strolled her way. He had a lazy grace when he wasn't angry or tense. A naturalness. Something that didn't come from a gym.

Alexis hadn't noticed him sitting in the old black truck parked on the street—half the population of this country town owned trucks. She glanced that way, wondering where Cliff was. The boy leaned out the window, looking bored. He didn't wave. She supposed he was still miffed with her.

"Yes. I suppose I'd better call someone. I don't believe there's a dealership in town for my car."

"I know a little about mechanics."

"Ah…yes. I suppose you do." In her opinion, most men arrogantly assumed they knew about motors and that women had no clue.

"Don't know if I can help. Small engines are my specialty."

"Sorry." She felt her cheeks flush. Of course he might know something about motors. She'd forgotten what his business was. "I hadn't thought…"

"Let me take a look-see."

"All right. That's very kind of you." On the playground adjoining the parking lot, Alexis heard the *thump-thump* of a basketball hitting the pavement. High school kids often used the grounds after school.

J.D. leaned past her, bending to the button inside her car and popping the hood. She stepped out of his way, murmuring, "Thank you."

"I haven't done anything yet."

A disembodied voice backed by static began to give out information: *"North on old Chaney Road…they need an ambulance…"*

Looking for the source, she spotted a two-way radio clipped to J.D.'s belt. He ignored it and didn't respond.

"Are you on an emergency response team?" she asked idly. Home-grown resources were good to know, and she filed away the knowledge in her teacher's mental file.

"Volunteer fireman. Not much need this past year, though, since Sunny Creek raised enough money to go with a couple of full-timers."

She heard the slam of the truck door. Cliff ran over and leaned under the yawning hood. His dark hair in his eyes, he nudged closer and hitched himself higher, almost crawling into the engine.

"Move, Cliff," J.D. muttered, though not unkindly.

Cliff's attention didn't last long. The boy soon wandered over to watch the ballplayers. Another youth streamed by on his skateboard, instantly engaging Cliff's interest.

"Do you know what's wrong?" Alexis asked. As old as the car was, the problem might be anything. She only prayed it wouldn't cost an arm to have fixed.

"Um…there's a break in the radiator hose."

"Uh-oh. How hard is that to fix?"

"Can't. You need a new one."

"Can I get one tonight?"

"Probably not. Don't worry about it. Cliff and I can run you home, and I'll come by in the morning and put a new one on for you."

He sounded competent and unexpectedly kind, but she wasn't too sure if she should accept his offer. This was a small town. People noticed when a teacher didn't arrive home in her own vehicle. They'd raise an eyebrow if a teacher became friends with a single father.

Yet she didn't relish walking the nearly two miles to her apartment tonight.

"Well…" Alexis glanced toward the school building. She could always beg a ride with Mrs. Henderson, the principal. Her car was in the lot, so she was still there. Yet who knew when Lavinia would be ready to leave?

"Cliff!" J.D. called, seeming to take for granted that she had accepted his offer. "Let's go."

Though they could see him trailing after the skate-boarder, Cliff didn't respond.

"Da— Um—" J.D. caught himself, giving her a rueful glance, letting her know she was the reason. Humor edged his mouth when he checked his language. "Drat, the boy. He ignores me all too often." J.D. raised his voice. "Cliff!"

"It's really kind of you to help, Mr. Sullivan, but I don't want to put you out." She wasn't sure it was the thing to do—letting him know where she lived. Although, in this small town it wouldn't take much detective work to find her—if someone really wanted to know. "You have your shop to get back to, I'm sure. And Cliff to take care of. Why don't I just—"

But her thought was interrupted when Cliff finally headed toward them. J.D. jerked his chin toward the truck and gestured for her to move.

"Just hold on to your patience, Miss Richmond, and climb in." J.D. held the truck door wide, handing Cliff onto the bench seat with ease. Then he held out a hand to her.

It would be ridiculous to refuse. Of course it would.

"We'll have you home in no time," he said. "Five minutes more away from my shop right now won't make a difference. I'll be open a little later anyway, since it's Friday night."

"Oh...um..." she muttered, contemplating the vehicle. The aged truck no longer had a step up. The only way she'd make it into that seat was to elevate her skirt high enough to give herself the mobility she needed to climb. But to refuse would be totally ungracious.

"Thank you." Throwing modesty to the winds, she hiked her purse to her shoulder, tossed her book bag before her, then lifted her skirt above her knees. She hadn't a hand left to grab anything to pull herself up.

His hand slipped under her elbow as she stepped up to reach the truck floor. For half an instant, she felt his warm breath on her cheek. Then she was up on the black leather seat next to Cliff.

"I do appreciate it," she said, turning just as his eyes lifted from her legs. His mouth softened as his gaze skittered away. She tugged her skirt back to her knees, feeling her cheeks flush like a teenager's.

She hadn't blushed in years.

"But if you don't mind—" she gently cleared her throat "—let me out at Fifth and Dogwood, please. I'm expected at a friend's house."

That should do it. He needn't know that she planned to spend her Friday evening with eighty-eight-year-old Mrs. Nelson.

He needn't think she was flirting with him, either.

Chapter Three

Early the next morning, Alexis shoved her feet into her running shoes, tied the laces, then twisted her ponytail under a royal-blue baseball cap. Bending, she engaged in a few stretches. Walking the less than two miles to school wasn't normally a problem. She'd done it several times last autumn, skipping through bright leaves while dreaming of her wedding plans. Plans that, over the winter, had fallen apart like a handful of dry sand tossed into the wind.

Lately she'd done no more than a desultory lunchtime stroll around the school playground. She had checked her personal disappointment at the door, hiding it behind bright smiles and teasing encouragement as she sauntered among the children. She drew the line at letting her negative emotions affect her school performance. Her kids needed all her positive energies.

Past time to put all that behind her, she mused, and to move on with her life. The physical exercise was good for her. She revved up her resolve. Last night's half-mile walk home from Mrs. Nelson's had been a snap.

It's a good time to talk with You, Lord.... she prayed now.

Switching a few items from her purse to a fanny pack, she tossed her cell phone on her bedside table. No outside distractions today. No chattering children nor classroom demands.

Changing seasons always reminds me of Your design for our personal changes, Father. I've been lax in my devotions lately. Please forgive me and help me know which direction You want me to pursue now that I'm single again. This is the second time I've nearly married the wrong choice for me. With all the mistakes I've made in choosing the wrong men in my life, I don't think I know any longer.

Sunshine drifted through budding trees to dapple the old sidewalk with shadow lace. It caught her fancy, bringing a smile to her lips. Alexis felt her heart lift in appreciation of the morning's beauty. Unable to help herself, she dawdled and admired the blossoming crocus in the yard nearest the school.

On this lazy spring Saturday, she expected most people to have a late start to their day. Finding J.D. in the school parking lot before her surprised her.

She quickened her step. His long, lean back was bent over her motor, and she could see only the curve of his face. He wore a dark, aged T-shirt that stretched along his shoulders and biceps as he moved. It stirred her senses. He reminded her of a calendar she once had in college that featured gorgeous blue-collar males. Firemen. Cops. Construction workers. All clothed and tastefully done, but nonetheless shining examples of male beauty.

Swallowing hard, she silently lamented, *Lord, this isn't helping. Why can't I see attraction in the right man for a change? I didn't even think Ron was this cute at first, and he had a few of the qualities I've been looking for. This guy is so off-the-mark for me....*

From what she could see, he didn't fit a single thing she wanted in a life mate. Short-tempered. Short on advanced education. Limited horizons.

Although to be fair, she didn't think J. D. Sullivan short on intelligence—he just didn't apply it to help himself much.

She had a mental list of the qualities, interests and goals she wanted—hoped and prayed—to share with a husband. Truth be known, she had a written list, too, one she'd made out at twenty. And revised at twenty-five. Now she'd have to look at it again, she supposed.

But all in all, there was something different about this man. J. D. Sullivan had an element she had yet to put her finger on.

He glanced up at that moment. In the sunlight, his brown eyes glinted with golden sparks. His mouth moved. Not in a smile exactly, but with an involuntary acknowledgment of her presence.

It was quickly hidden before he said, "Almost got it done."

She glanced away, letting her gaze rove the school

yard. "Where's Cliff? I thought he'd be here with you this morning."

"He's right—" J.D. stopped what he was doing and shrugged. After glancing around, he let out a disgusted breath. "Well, he was there a minute ago. On his skateboard."

He stuck his head back under the hood, mumbling. "That boy is just asking for it. I'm likely to lock him in his room and throw away the key if he keeps this up. Told him to stay close by, but he keeps disappearing on me. Kid can't seem to follow the simplest orders."

A flare of irritation shot up her body. She tried to tamp it down, realizing she did not know the circumstances of their situation. This adjustment was extremely difficult on both of them, and it touched a sympathetic chord in her. But…how dare J.D. treat his son with such flippant lack of concern? Didn't he love the child at all? Didn't he care what the boy got himself into? Where he went?

Cliff must feel the loss of his mother keenly. How could the child cope with a father who rebuffed him?

Alexis felt so blessed. She'd had a loving set of parents and two older sisters to nurture her through childhood. They accepted her completely. Plus she had a plethora of extended family to fill her life. There never was a time when she hadn't felt wanted and cherished. Even after her recent breakup with Ron, she'd never doubted her family's love, nor her Lord's.

She leaned against the car door, silently praying, *Father, give me patience…and wisdom….*

Perhaps that was the major problem. Just maybe neither of these two felt loved. According to the paperwork she had, this father and son had only each other. And since they'd just been reunited after a five-year absence, they were near strangers. Perhaps J.D. didn't know how to love his son. Or even know what it was to love.

You're the teacher....

Her breath came sharply and lodged uncomfortably just under her breastbone. J.D glanced her way, his expression quizzical.

"Cliff is probably on the other playground," she said abruptly. Turning on her heel, Alexis went to search for him. "I'll find him."

She sprinted around the building to the small playground in back of the original section of the school. Then she rounded the corner, seeing no one. She wasn't surprised. This field was seldom used anymore because most of the classes found it too small.

She heard children's voices and noisy activity from up the way. Crossing the street, she hurried along the old broken sidewalk. Still yards distant, she spotted three boys.

It wasn't a friendly scene.

Skateboard raised high above his head, Randy Brown's irritated voice floated out to her. Alexis remembered him from last year, her first year of teaching in Sunny Creek. The boy was two grades higher than Cliff, half a head taller and a bit of a bully. He was yelling in strident tones, "You don't know nothin', brat, so just stuff it."

Jason Kell, also two years older and even taller than Randy, stood with arms crossed, glaring at Cliff.

When she strolled up to them, he rolled his eyes in distaste, letting her know his opinion of the younger boy.

Cliff had his back to her. He didn't seem to notice their ire. He was talking a mile a minute. "I do so. I can do lots of tricks. I watched how they do it out in California. They're better'n any of you guys. They have a monster track. I'm going to be a champion and stuff, just like them. You wait to see."

Her first instinct was that she'd arrived just in time. It was clear that Cliff had worn out his welcome.

As she smiled at the older boys, she saw recognition of her teacher's status flash across Randy's face.

"Hi, guys."

They mumbled a hello. Cliff kept talking.

"Cliff?"

He glanced over his shoulder impatiently. "Yeah?"

She held out her hand. "Let's go. Your dad wants you."

"He's busy doing something else," he protested. He dropped his skateboard, stepping up and pushing off to ride the length of the concrete drive. Away from her.

"Yes, but he wants you now." She firmed her tone. "Come along, we need to go."

The skateboard hit a bump and tipped. Cliff jumped off awkwardly, barely avoiding a fall. Randy and Jason snickered.

Cliff glared with all the ferocity of a wolf pup.

Alexis hid her sigh. Cliff already sported skinned knees, so she suspected he'd taken a number of recent falls. She didn't see much of his father's grace in the boy's movements. He would have to grow into that, she supposed. It might take a while.

Meantime, he was ripe for all the teasing grief he'd already encountered. If only he didn't invite it.

She casually moved toward him, not wanting to cause alarm. Yet her movement held command.

"I don't see why I have to leave." Cliff's tone was contentious. "He's looking at your car."

"That's right. But he's almost through and he needs you." She tipped her head, giving her statement additional authority. "Now, let's go."

Cliff's face took on all the aspects of the proverbial Missouri mule. But after a moment, he picked up his board and followed her up the terrace to the playground. "I don't see why I can't stay here…"

Out of earshot of the other boys, she slowed her step to let him walk alongside of her. "I know you like to ride your board, Cliff," she said in sympathy. "There will be other times when you can practice."

"But I wanted to show those guys." His eyes, even darker that his dad's, took on a soulful, puppy dog despair.

Feeling a rush of compassion, Alexis reached out and ruffled his hair with affection. "Maybe you will. So…how long have you had your skateboard?"

Although still pouting, Cliff seemed to relax. After a moment, he moved closer, making an effort to match his step with hers while he chattered about the thrills of skateboarding.

As they arrived at the car, J.D. wiped his hands and glanced up. His bright gaze questioned, but he asked nothing about where she'd found the boy.

"Is it ready?" Alexis asked.

Cliff let his board clang to the asphalt and shot away.

"Nope. Needs more than just a new water hose. You should have it checked over thoroughly before you drive it."

"Oh…" Disappointment washed over her. She'd have to arrange for a few rides until her car was running again. She couldn't afford to trade this one in just yet. "What's wrong with it now?"

"Don't know for sure. But Bill, from the car repair over at Fifth and Main, most likely can tell you. Reckon you can get a loaner from him if you need to."

"Oh, well. That will have to do, I guess."

"I'm hungry," Cliff complained, coming up to them. "You said we'd eat real soon."

"You haven't had breakfast?" Alexis asked.

"Nothing in the house but boring old cereal," Cliff complained.

"Better than nothing, Cliff," J.D. stated. "If you were really hungry, you'd eat it."

Alexis glanced at her watch. Almost nine. Around them, the neighborhood activity had begun to pick up.

"Are you late in opening your shop?" she asked J.D. What did those initials stand for, anyway?

"Not really." He picked up the last of his tools and slammed the hood closed. "Don't open till ten most days in the off-season. Come summer, I'll open at nine on Saturdays."

The day yawned before her, long and empty. Oh, there were always household chores and laundry to do. School papers to grade. But she'd counted on driving to the outlying shopping center to find a new spring outfit, and now that she couldn't do that, she felt she couldn't stand to be indoors on such a fine spring day.

"Then, let me buy you two breakfast," she offered impulsively. "It's the least I can do to thank you."

J.D.'s mouth tightened as he bent to his toolbox. He took out some cleaning gel and squirted a dollop into his palm. "That's not necessary. Just helping you out."

"I appreciate that, to be sure." Alexis watched J.D. rub his palms together, then smooth the gel over his fingers. He took particular care around his nails, she noted.

"But I'm hungry, too," she insisted. "And Cliff has worked up quite an appetite, I'll bet." She turned to the boy. "Do you like pancakes?"

"Uh-huh." Cliff gave her a curious look, bright with anticipation.

"Then, how about the Pancake House in the old part of town? They offer steak and eggs, too. A hearty breakfast to last the day is always good. I'd say you earned it."

She waited for J.D.'s answer, noticing the gleam in

his eyes, and wondered what she'd let herself in for. But what could it hurt? It was only breakfast, and they all needed to eat. Besides, this was for Cliff as much as anything. If she could do something to make Cliff's adjustment to his new environment easier, then she helped herself as well, right? He'd do better in class.

"Sounds okay by me," J.D. said. He flashed a smile that sent her tummy into a wild, dancing dip. Oh, mercy… What had she gotten herself into?

There was no way she could back out now. She'd feel a fool. She'd simply make the best of it.

J.D. closed his toolbox and placed it in his truck. Then he held the door wide. "Hop in. After breakfast we can run by Bill's place and see when he can work on the car."

Whether the truck was ever meant to accommodate a small person, Alexis had no idea. The step up left her no dignity, she mused as she stared at it. But at least this time she was better prepared.

His hand came under her elbow, lifting her into the front seat. Cliff climbed in beside her, his thin body taking more space than she'd suspect. J.D. slid in under the wheel, his shoulder brushing hers as he turned the ignition key. A masculine fragrance tickled her nose, making her wonder what soap he used.

She tried to scoot closer to Cliff's side of the bench seat, but there wasn't much room.

"That'll do it."

That's what she was afraid of.…

"By the way…" she began, unable to help herself

as he paused before pulling out on the street. "Just what does the J.D. stand for?"

This time his grin held a definite impish tilt. "Why, it's James Dean, ma'am. After that fifties movie star best known for his rebel roles."

Chapter Four

"**H**i there, J.D." The perky brunette waitress's blue eyes lit in a coltish glance. The twenty-something young woman seemed vaguely familiar, but Alexis couldn't place her.

Alexis wasn't surprised at someone knowing her companion. She'd long ago discovered the truth of all small towns: those born and raised there seemed to know each other. Or *about* each other at least.

Neither was she surprised that J.D. had his female fans. She imagined he had quite a few—though at the moment he seemed not to notice.

"Hi yourself, Tina." J.D. returned the smile with a casual nod.

Cliff spotted the video machines in the back corner and made a beeline toward them.

"You haven't been around much lately." With a flashing glance, Tina let him know how much she'd missed him.

Alexis listened to the murmurs of the busy restaurant and then intercepted a curious glance from a man sitting at the counter.

She bit at her lower lip, wondering who else noticed them. What had she expected? But if she'd realized J.D. was so well known here, she'd have suggested one of the new places out on the highway.

Just forget it, she told herself. *Living with a bit of gossip is part of living in a small town.*

Yet she'd have a lot of explaining to do eventually when her fellow teachers heard of this morning's events. *This is for a student....* she mentally practiced her excuse. *The child just lost his mom. He needs some help adjusting to his new home...his new environment....*

They were real reasons—not merely excuses—but it didn't quite explain the social interaction in which she now found herself. Yet what else could she do? The child needed help. That had nothing to do with how attractive she found the father.

Alexis discreetly followed Cliff. The boy grabbed the joystick of the first machine, making the buzzing noises of an airplane.

"Been busy," J.D. replied to Tina. "You can tell your dad I found the parts he wants for his old two-stroke engine. They'll come in by next weekend."

"Sure, J.D., I'll tell him. D'you want your usual place at the counter?"

"Let's have that back booth this morning, Tina. There's three of us."

Alexis glanced over her shoulder in time to catch Tina's surprise. "Oh, sure, okay...."

So not everyone yet knew about Cliff coming to live with his dad.

"Dad, can I have some money?" Cliff called across the restaurant. A few heads turned their way in curiosity. J.D. nodded to one or two on his way to the back booth.

Well, the whole town would know now.

"I'll get you some menus," Tina said brightly.

I'll bet Tina knows exactly what J.D. will order, Alexis mused, *without looking at a menu.*

"Come sit down, Cliff," J.D. said. "Let's order first."

"That's a good idea," Alexis said. She put her hand on the boy's shoulder to lightly guide him toward the back corner booth. "I'm starved and I hear the blueberry pancakes are wonderful here."

Cliff slid into the booth next to his dad, leaning his head into his hand. He stared at Tina. "Are you my dad's girlfriend?"

"Uh, no." The young woman started, then blushed to the roots of her hair. "My boyfriend...he...isn't from around here."

"Cliff, can't you keep your mouth shut?" J.D. said.

"I only asked. What's wrong with that?"

Alexis immediately felt sorry for the girl. It seemed obvious to her that Tina had a crush on J.D. But was J.D. aware of that?

"That's none of your business, Cliff." J.D. narrowed his eyes and spoke firmly. "But for your information, her dad and I are good fishing buddies. That's all.'' He turned to the young waitress. ''Sorry, Tina. Guess I have to teach my son some manners. Let's order.''

Cliff lost interest. As Tina took their orders, he began to swing his foot, kicking the seat.

''Cliff!'' J.D. said, his tone firm.

''What?''

''Stop kicking.''

The boy stopped, but only a moment passed before he grabbed the salt and pepper shakers to march them across the table with clacking noises. Without comment, Alexis reached across and took the shakers out of his hands. She gently set them aside.

A grateful flash from J.D.'s dark gaze sent a warm glow to her heart. Along with it came all kinds of other messages of awareness…his vulnerability being most prominent. Her fingertips itched to touch his hand in reassurance. As a parent, he seemed totally helpless. But surely any parent would know how difficult a special-needs child could be….

That was the major problem, though, she was beginning to understand. J.D. didn't know, he hadn't a clue. She opened her mouth to offer something to soothe him, but he'd slipped away somewhere in his thoughts.

You're a washout, boy, came an old refrain inside J.D.'s head. *Can't you do anything right?* An echo from too many yesterdays, painful and loud in the household where he'd grown up. His own father had shown little patience with a son who would rather spend time at an auto repair shop than school, home or studies.

He was still a washout, he guessed. Melanie had told him so often enough. As a husband. As a father.

He immediately cut off that line of thought. So he wasn't good husband material. What did that matter? He didn't have to be, since he had no intention of getting married again. And as a dad, it was up to him now, wasn't it? And given time, he'd learn to deal with his son, learn to be a better father than he had had.

Tina filled their coffee cups, then left. J.D. leaned back and glanced at Alexis. She'd pulled off her ball cap, letting her ponytail dangle. He had the urge to finger it, to see if it was as soft as it looked. But this was his son's teacher…and her sympathetic blue gaze held more than a little speculation.

He shifted uncomfortably to stare silently at the far wall. He didn't know what to say next. This wasn't like a date, now was it?

"I seem to remember seeing Tina at our church service," Alexis said by way of conversation. "She sits with a girlfriend when the college kids are home on break."

"Hmm," J.D. answered.

"We have an active teen group. But there's not many of Tina's age around on a normal Sunday."

He stirred his coffee, working on thinking about how much he had to do at his shop and not how

Alexis's hair reminded him of corn silk. Or how dumb she must think he was.

"I've heard that once kids graduate high school here, most of them leave either for college or to work in the larger cities," she continued. "Not too much in this town by way of employment."

J.D. secretly studied Alexis's slim fingers. Ringless today. Light polish over short, well-shaped nails.

She made small talk to fill his silence, he knew. Something he wasn't good at anytime, but especially not with this kind of woman. Nothing in common. Anyway, he'd never felt the need to constantly fill the air with the sound of his own voice. Unless he discussed engines, or fishing and the state of the lakes. Nah—small talk with women always felt too awkward.

Anyway, he preferred to simply look at a teacher; teachers had always given him a headache. He didn't see a need to talk to one if a guy didn't have to.

And looking at this one in particular was okay. Actually, a pure number ten on the pleasure scale. And if he forgot she was a teacher and thought of her merely as a female....

He liked the way her mouth moved when she talked. If she taught any of those extension classes the high school offered adults, he might just be tempted to take one.

He suddenly noticed Alexis's blue gaze fastened on him expectantly. A softness, sweet beyond sweet potato pie, filled her gaze. A shaft of out-and-out pleasure shot through him as straight as a well-aimed dart.

If he didn't watch it, she'd send him into a tailspin of wants—and where would that get him? On the no-where road. She was his son's teacher. Nothing more.

Small talk…what was it she had said? About the jobs available in town?

"Seasonal stuff," J.D. answered absently. "Most years are good, but not always steady."

Cliff whistled tunelessly. Neither melodiously nor under his breath.

"Cliff." J.D. let out a frustrated sigh and rubbed his temple with his thumb. The kid would make a sphinx yelp in protest.

"Can I play the videos while we wait?"

"Sure, why not." He felt weak for giving in to his son's constant demands, but he'd had about enough of frazzled nerves for the morning. Beyond that, he and his son hadn't yet made friends with each other.

More proof that, as a father, he was a dud.…

He dug into his pocket and pulled out change, then counted out all the quarters he had. "Make that do."

Cliff grabbed the coins and scooted out of the booth.

J.D. sat without speaking. He savored the next mo-ment of quiet before a creeping awareness of guilt snaked up his consciousness. What kind of a father was he, to never want his son around? To feel no closeness to the boy?

And whose fault is that? You could have gone to California to see him. Could have sought joint cus-tody. Could have demanded proof of Melanie's claims that Cliff wasn't yours.…

That issue had been put to rest once and for all in Melanie's last letter. The one she'd written as she lay dying. And there was always DNA testing these days. But he didn't need it. Cliff was his, all right. He saw too much of himself in the boy to doubt it. No, the fault was his.

"Guess I'll never be a good dad."

"Why do you say that?" Alexis asked.

He hadn't really intended on getting into a discussion with Miss Richmond on this subject right now; he didn't want her to dig too deep.

But he did need help. Only God knew how much.

He swallowed the last of his coffee and looked around to catch Tina's eye for a refill, to no avail. Tina chatted with a customer at the far end of the counter. He couldn't find any excuse for postponement from that direction.

"Can't make the kid mind," he finally said. On his side of the table he shoved his knife and fork from place to place. It was embarrassing to voice all his failures. He wasn't used to it. "He doesn't listen and I lose my temper. I have no patience."

"James…"

It came softly from her lips, implying intimacy. Caught off guard, he glanced up. She held his gaze and wouldn't let go. He felt his stomach go south.

"You don't mind if I call you James, do you? Instead of J.D.?"

"Nah," he mumbled. "Guess not."

"Well, James, may I ask you a few questions?"

Amusement tugged at the corners of his mouth.

Questions? She hadn't asked permission before now. "Teachers do, don't they?" He smiled.

"Yes, I suppose they do," she said ruefully. "Often. Okay, since you don't mind… Did Cliff listen to you when you and his mother were together?"

"Nope." Now he felt worse. He hadn't thought much about that before. "Never did, I guess. Even when he was two or three. I couldn't… Guess I never got the hang of being a good dad."

He'd left too much for Melanie to take care of while he worked two jobs to support them. At the time, he'd thought that enough.

"Now I don't know what to do next," he admitted, ashamed that he couldn't seem to find a pathway that worked.

"Parenting is always one step at a time," she commented. "Nobody learns it in one fell swoop. Besides, I don't know any perfect parents. All of them make a mistake or two."

"Yeah, but I…" His pent-up breath pained him as he let it go. "I have to admit I haven't been around much for the boy. None at all these past years."

"Why was that?" she asked. Her gentleness in asking the question wiped out whatever sense of intrusion he might normally have felt.

"Seemed easy enough when that's what his mother wanted." He shrugged. The excuses he'd used all these years no longer seemed valid, even to himself. "Didn't see much sense in letting Cliff see us at our worst. Fighting all the time. But if I'd taken more interest, maybe Cliff wouldn't be such a mess now."

"James, you couldn't have prevented all of Cliff's problems. Even the best of parents can have children with a hyperactivity disorder or some kind of learning disability."

"What do you mean?"

"I mean…now the complete evaluation hasn't yet been done, but I think your son has Attention Deficit Hyperactivity Disorder—ADHD. He's a child who simply can't pay attention or control his impulses."

"You mean, he's not just spoiled?"

Alexis chuckled. "Oh, he's a bit spoiled, all right. I suspect he's been given his own way all too often. He does seem to think he's entitled to indulge his every whim. But it's not beyond repair."

"What you're telling me is…this isn't all my fault?" A sudden hope sparked his thoughts. He sat straighter and leaned forward.

"Not at all. He simply needs specialized teaching. Direction for studies, specific direction for his social exchanges."

"Specific directions?" His heart beat with an out-of-sequence *ping*. What she was telling him made real sense.

"Like how? What…what can *I* do?"

"For one thing, you can set firm, consistent boundaries for him at home, then stick to them. But…not with spanking, please. There are other disciplines to use. We'll do the same for him at school. We'll do our best to teach him to focus on his studies."

"You think he'll improve then?"

"I think there's a one-hundred-percent probability."

"What else?"

"I think…" She hesitated, tucking her chin in and biting her lip. "I don't want to step over the line here, James. I'm Cliff's teacher, not a psychologist."

"Tell me. Please. I don't need any of the usual professional jargon."

"It's only my opinion."

"And I asked for it, Alexis." All at once it didn't feel at all awkward to address her by her given name. And more to the point, she didn't seem to notice. He watched the way she pressed her lips together, the way she folded her hands in front of her, teacherlike, making up her mind to say what she honestly thought.

"Have you talked with him, yet, about the loss of his mother?"

That one surprised him. "Not more than a few words. He doesn't seem to want to talk about it."

Alexis thought about that a moment. "Perhaps that will come later. After he trusts you more. Meanwhile, I think Cliff is in need of lots of love."

"Love? I love the boy."

"Yes, I'm sure you do. But you need to show him some affection, James."

"Affection?"

"Hugs. A pat on the back. Show that you care."

Hugs? Cliff was nine years old. Hugging a boy child of nine seemed— Wasn't that too old? But he could manage pats on the back, he supposed.

Tina was heading their way with their order.

"I'd bet Cliff would even still welcome a nighttime tuck-in before he sleeps," Alexis said.

"Tuck him in?" he mumbled. "At nine?" That was really stretching it, but…

"Here you go," Tina said, putting dishes on the table.

Alexis smiled with an encouragement that lit his heart like a Roman candle. What did he have to lose by trying her methods?

"Uh…time to eat." He rose and strode over to the video machines. Placing a hand on his son's shoulder, he murmured next to his ear, then nodded toward their booth. He said nothing when Cliff raced recklessly across the room.

Alexis smiled a welcome for Cliff, nodding to his pancakes. Maybe she'd suggested they have breakfast together as a way of doing her teacher thing, J.D. mused, but they'd covered more ground than just his son's problems. She acted like a friend.

More than a friend?

An image rose in his mind of a bedtime routine. He wouldn't mind being tucked into bed himself. If the tucker was Alexis.

It made him smile. A smile that remained as he slipped into the booth.

The quizzical glance she gave him was worth twice the price of breakfast. His smile broadened. Maybe he could get into this teacher-parent thing after all.

Chapter Five

Cliff dug into his backpack, hauling out books, grubby loose papers, a sports magazine and a package of cheese crackers, before he pulled out the envelope Alexis had sent home with him Friday night. Alexis had written a short account of Cliff's week at school. It was only a slim margin more successful than those first few days.

He flipped it onto her desk, then ambled toward his seat.

"Thank you, Cliff," Alexis said. A piece of popcorn tumbled from the envelope as she picked it up, making her smile. She pulled out the note. As he'd done twice before, James had responded on the back of the paper.

Funny, how eager she felt to read what had been up to now only a sentence or two.

Ah, progress felt sweet. Even this tiny bit of progress. This was a whole paragraph.

"We had a half-decent weekend," James wrote. "Cliff came to the shop with me on Saturday. Found him unexpectedly at the top of the high ladder once, looking at the inventory on the top shelf. Followed your advice. Didn't yell at him. Asked him to tell me what was there, then thanked him for his help. He came down when I asked him to. So far, popcorn seems to do him as a substitute snack to candy. Thanks again, Miss Richmond."

He'd signed it with his full name.

She rubbed her thumb over the *James Dean Sullivan.* It summoned a mental image of that half smile and the cocky gleam shooting from his glance. Oh, my! It seemed a long week plus a weekend since their breakfast together.

Beyond that, the thought that some of her suggestions were successful for Cliff and his father was heady stuff. It warmed her heart. Alexis's initial reaction was to sit and immediately respond. Instead, she called the class to order and began her school day.

Yet the glow from James's note threaded her whole morning, and by afternoon she wondered if she dare invite James Dean Sullivan and his son to the spring picnic her Bible Study group had on their calendar for the next Sunday afternoon. Her study group mostly consisted of couples, but a few singles like herself attended. The picnic was to be a family affair. Kids of all ages would be there, and hopefully Cliff could find a friend. He sure needed one.

It seemed a very personal invitation.

Too personal? she asked herself.

She frowned slightly, struggling with it. Surely it would be fine. Why not? She didn't think they ever went to church because Cliff had talked of sleeping late on Sunday. And James could only benefit by joining a Bible Study. Cliff needed the kind of love only the Lord could provide. Why wouldn't it be okay to ask them to a worship service, then the picnic following? It was the kind thing to do.

Oh, sure, that was her reason all right, she thought in disgust. It was the kind thing to do? Who was she fooling? It still remained a personal invitation.

But was it really wise to make this so personal? It would feed the gossips.

Yet wise or not, Cliff and James needed more than they had right now. A church fellowship could only help them further cement their relationship.

It all made perfect sense to her, but still she should leave it to James, she mused. She wondered about his spiritual health. He'd said nothing about his relationship with God during their few talks. She'd already made the suggestion once to him to find a church to attend. There was a fine line between helpfulness and intrusion, she knew, and for some people, this was very private business.

Besides, they had nothing personal in common at all—no matter how sexy the guy's grin was.

Yet an hour later, she knew she couldn't leave it alone, either. Just before the last bell of the day, she gave in and scribbled a note of invitation for Cliff to take to James. Before she could second-guess herself, she included her home phone number.

Overstepping herself or not, it still felt right for her to help a student who needed it. And his father.

At home that night Alexis filled her evening with reading student papers and giving her tiny kitchen an extra clean. She kept her cell phone close by as she hauled two loads of laundry to the basement and completed it.

James didn't call.

At eleven she climbed into bed, refusing to admit disappointment. Why should she? Inviting him to the church picnic had been only an impulse....

At five minutes past seven the next morning, the phone rang. This early in the day, a phone call usually meant something extra going on at school, or an emergency.

At the point of gathering her hair into a ponytail, she clasped two hair clips between her teeth and tucked the phone under her chin. "Hello," she mumbled.

"'Lo. This is J.D." His voice held an early-morning huskiness, which sent goose bumps skittering across her arms.

Her heart hit a bump in its rhythm. The hair clips went flying as she spat them out. "Uh, hello, James. What's up?"

"Didn't get your note till this morning."

"Oh. Didn't Cliff do his homework?"

"Uh, yeah. Sort of. Didn't get it finished, I'm afraid. My fault. I had a shipment of parts come in that I had to take care of, so I... Sorry. Didn't get home till nearly midnight. I didn't have time to check it till this morning.''

"I see. Well, we'll have to work on it during study time.''

"Okay. Thanks. About Sunday…''

"Yes?''

"We'll come.''

Her heart bumped again, then settled down, racing only a tad. This was definitely good for Cliff. For them both. The idea of spending more time with James didn't hover as a great chore, either.

"Great.'' She was glad he couldn't see her. See the smile she couldn't hide. "I think you know where the church is?''

"Yeah, sure do.'' His tone picked up enthusiasm. "We'll be there on time. Should we bring something for the picnic?''

"Not this time. There'll be enough food for an army. It's out at the Bender farm by a creek that feeds into the lake. Cliff can bring his fishing pole if he wants to.''

There was a slight hesitation before he said, "I don't think Cliff is into fishing, but I'll pack a couple of rods just in case. One for you, too.''

"Uh, well, I don't really fish.''

"Then, I'll teach you.''

"I hate to tell you this, James, being a teacher and all—'' Alexis moistened her lips "—but I don't relish picking up live worms, much less sticking them on a hook.''

His deep chuckle tickled her ear. She had a sinking feeling she shouldn't have told him.

"You don't have to handle live worms, Alexis. I'll take care of the bait for you."

"Thank goodness." She rushed on to say, "I wouldn't want Cliff to see his teacher freaking out over such a little thing as picking up a worm. But honestly, when I was a kid, science was my worst subject because I couldn't bring myself to touch anything slimy."

"And you haven't outgrown that aversion, hmm?" His tone held a note of amusement.

A sense of horror stole over her. "You're not going to hold that over my head, are you?"

"It's mighty tempting. I can just imagine what Cliff would do with that piece of information about our Miss Richmond."

Could he imagine Cliff using it, or himself? What kind of child had James been? As mischievous as she suspected? Something in her growing knowledge of him told her he may have caused his mother to go gray early.

"It wouldn't help much in class, either," she muttered.

"Don't worry. I won't cause you any trouble in class. It's only— Never mind. I'll see you Sunday."

They rang off, leaving Alexis's ears ringing with James's chortles.

That may have been a big mistake—her honesty over handling worms. She shook her head and grabbed her brush, then left her hair to hang about her face without clips. She was likely to be late for school.

She parked in her usual spot and exited her car just as Lori Donato, the regular fifth-grade teacher, parked next to her.

"Hi, Alexis," Lori called as she slid her plump form from her car and reached for a canvas bag. "I've been meaning to catch up with you. Do you have a free period today? We need to discuss the field trip up to the Truman Museum if we're going to do it next month."

"You're right, we should make some plans soon." Alexis hefted her own overly full briefcase and pocketed her keys. "How about during lunch?"

"That'll do. When—"

A familiar black truck slowed to an idle alongside them. It was impossible not to notice him. James hung one arm out his window.

Cliff slid out the other side.

"Morning, Miss Richmond," James said with a smile as deliberate as four beats to a measure. Somehow, after their recent interaction, his formal address sounded more like a spoken intimacy.

"Good morning." Alexis stepped closer to the truck, fighting the desire to let her own silly grin explode.

She glanced at Cliff as he rounded the truck, and her budding smile dwindled. The child sported droopy eyes. Had he been as late getting to bed as his dad? That would make for a trying day.

Keeping a school child up late…

Alexis tried to tamp down her vexation. Single parenting had its pitfalls and she didn't think James had any backup when he had to work late. Keeping his child with him at the shop was the lesser of two evils, she supposed, compared to leaving him at home alone.

From the few remarks Cliff had made, Alexis suspected that had been a problem in the past. The boy's mother had left him alone far too often to make a solitary meal on hot dogs, soda and chips, and then with no one to take notice, to put himself to bed. In spite of it all, James's choice to take Cliff to work with him was the better one.

"Hiya, Lori." James addressed the other teacher.

"Hi there, J.D." Lori spoke with familiarity. "How have you been? Heard about Cliff coming home to live with you. Sorry about Melanie. Are you making out all right these days?"

"Learning. With a little help from my friends...." His glance, warm with gratitude, rested on Alexis.

Lori's glance moved to Alexis, as well. "Uh, that's good. Can never have too many friends. And Miss Richmond is a good teacher."

Alexis clutched her bag tighter as a flush climbed her cheeks. "Thanks. But it's my job."

"That picnic is a terrific idea, Alexis," James said, reclaiming her attention. His hair appeared as tousled as Cliff's, and she wanted to ask him where his hairbrush had got to—only she rather liked it in its disheveled state. "Cliff and I can use the break."

The tall, thin figure of their district school superintendent, Mr. Fisher, appeared out of nowhere. The county was building new offices, but until they were complete, the district's temporary office was across from the school. They shared the parking lot.

"Good morning, ladies. Staff meeting at the last bell today, you recall."

Their school was losing their principal this year. Besides that, the entire district had been in something of a reorganization. From what Lori and Kathy, Alexis's assistant, told her, Mr. Fisher delighted in keeping his hand in it.

Mr. Fisher tossed an unsmiling nod toward James before he continued, pinning his gaze on Lori and Alexis as though they were the adversary. "I'd take it as a personal favor if you'd be on time."

"Sure, Mr. Fisher," Alexis said. "We'll be there."

"Uh-oh," Lori muttered as the superintendent hustled away. "He's in one of his moods. Guess it's time to stand and salute, so he knows we're paying attention."

James chuckled at Lori's impudent quip. Lori's dimples made an appearance as she tried to suppress her humor.

"Oh, fine." Alexis swallowed hers. Unsuccessfully, she guessed, because Lori laughed outright.

She cast a baleful glance between them. "What if one of the kids hears you?" Alexis complained. "I have enough to deal with in my classroom. How am I to teach my students respect for those in authority when they see you two rebels in action?"

James let his grin broaden and gunned his motor. "See you later, Alexis."

As James drove away, Lori fell into step beside her as they headed inside. "So…I see you and J.D. seem to have hit it off."

"As well we should. We're both concerned about Cliff," Alexis answered, halfway between feeling cautious and hopeful that it was true.

"Yeah, I am, too. Seriously." Then Lori's dimples showed up again, and she shot a teasing gleam Alexis's way. "But if I weren't already happily married to my Steven, I'd be real tempted to be actively concerned with J.D., too. He's one sexy dude."

"Uh, yeah, so I've heard. I'm, um, glad to know you're in Cliff's corner, Lori," Alexis said, ignoring the personal remark. She turned her head quickly, hoping Lori hadn't noticed the second flush of the morning flooding her face. "But now I have to get to class."

The anticipation of Sunday lasted with Alexis all week. It seemed so with James, as well. On Thursday, it permeated another note in reply to her comments on Cliff's progress.

"Told Cliff we wouldn't go to the picnic if he didn't pick up his stuff from the living room," it read. "He groused, but did a better job than usual. You're a genius. We should plan more than picnics."

More than picnics?

Alexis counted the days to this one.

James knew the Bender farm. Not a large acreage— the land was too hilly to raise much aside from cattle. But the Bender family had held it for about a hundred years and it had footage along a stream that emptied into the Lake of the Ozarks. No one occupied the old cottage on a full-time basis these days, but it still had some charm. It was a perfect place for a weekend retreat or a picnic, and of course he was looking forward to the social contact.

It seemed a very long time since he'd had anything close to a date. If he could count this as such. His rare hookups at the local nightspots didn't fall into that category either.

The church service was another matter. Late on Saturday night, he'd begun to worry about it. The church he'd attended as a child was rather formal in its approach to worship, and its members usually dressed up. He wasn't too sure about this one. Neither he nor Cliff owned a suit. He hadn't worn one in years.

He punched in Alexis's number. Any excuse to call her was a good one in his book. He hadn't seen her in days, and those brief notes simply weren't enough. He wanted a little flirtation to carry into his dreams after a long hard day. A hard week, in fact.

Who would have thought he'd be attracted to a teacher?

"Mmm…hello?"

"Did I wake you?"

"Uh…only a little." Her sleepy voice purred like a kitten. He silently grinned at the thought. He liked kittens. "I guess I dosed over school paperwork."

Where had she dozed? On a sofa? At a kitchen table? In bed?

He did his paperwork at the old wooden desk that

once belonged to his father—one of the few things he'd kept from the old house he'd inherited after his mom died a few years back. He recalled lots of evenings staring at his father's cold silence. His dad locked himself in an invisible cocoon at that desk while James struggled with his homework.

He turned away from it now. He wanted warmth and welcome, not aloof rejection. "Paperwork is usually the last thing I get to, as well."

"Is something the matter?" Her voice held concern.

"Not really." James shook off the somber memory. For once, Cliff had gone to bed without a fight and J.D. was tired of talking business. His purpose in phoning was to flirt just a bit before calling it a day. "Just wondered about the service tomorrow."

"What about it? You're not backing out, are you?" she asked.

"No, it's not that. I, um, just didn't have time to go shopping."

"Shopping? What has that to do with it?"

"I don't dress up much," he warned her. "No call to in my business."

"Is that all?" She sounded relieved.

For no particular reason, his spirits lifted. She wasn't being merely polite. She *wanted* him there.

"Well, it's nothing to worry about. Lots of worshipers dress in casual attire. Even jeans, and modest shorts during the summer."

"Really? That's a far cry from when I was a kid."

Actually, he had already known that. Most people coming to the lake for vacation didn't bother to dress up for anything, either. He also knew longtime towns-people sometimes dressed for church, but the mix would be about equal. He had simply wanted an excuse to keep her talking.

Without actually saying so, he'd given her the notion he never went to church. Which was the truth, he silently admitted. "I guess it's okay, then. A sport shirt will do?"

"Yes…James—" he thought the way she said his name gave it a whole new meaning, and he didn't care if no one ever called him J.D. again "—if you are nervous about coming, I'll wait outside on the steps for you."

"That's great with me. Cliff will be less wild, I'm thinking, with you there."

"Fine, then. I'll see you at a quarter to nine."

They'd be sitting together. Never mind that it would help with Cliff. J.D. wanted to sit by her side himself. He liked the idea that they'd be close enough to brush shoulders.

Punching the off button, he settled back in his chair. Then he rose and headed for a shower. This going to church might have a bigger payoff than he'd thought.

Chapter Six

On Sunday morning Alexis spent an extra thirty minutes getting ready, and still arrived at the church on time. She wore a new blue print dress in a silky texture—one she'd bought over spring break—and high-heeled sandals to match. Her hair flowed smoothly to barely touch her shoulders in a soft page-boy style she'd just adopted.

She waited at the top of the church steps, watching James and Cliff climb them. As he came toward her, James's gaze traveled upward from her high heels, paused at her narrow waist, then rose to stare into her eyes. His sparked with appreciation.

Funny how pleased she felt. James may not match the academic achievements of the men in whom she'd been interested in the past, but his male reflexes would score a thousand percent in anyone's book.

A church greeter welcomed James and Cliff. Alexis

smiled her own reception and led the way into the sanctuary.

She wasn't surprised by the friendly greetings J.D. received from people who knew him, although she thought a few church members were caught off guard seeing him there. James even seemed a tad embarrassed by one or two. Their genuineness made up for any undue curiosity.

She and J.D. slid into the pew the usher showed them, Cliff between them. Alexis heard a faint whooshing breath and glanced at James as she settled back. Was that an overexpectant or apprehensive gaze he sent her? She couldn't tell.

He merely smiled and gave a slight shake of his head.

Cliff's behavior was fine until it was time for the sermon. He squirmed after a few minutes of listening, unable to sit quietly. Prepared, Alexis pulled out a packet of pipe cleaners. For the next thirty minutes Cliff was quietly captivated by all the shapes he could form with them.

James watched his son for a few moments, then, as the pastor gave the scripture passage for the day, he reached into his pocket for a ballpoint pen. He scribbled on the back of his program, then slipped it across to her. Cliff, focusing on his new creation, paid no attention.

Alexis read the short sentence. "Sheer genius."

"Elementary," she scribbled in return.

"Maybe. But—?" came back to her.

"You're learning," she wrote.

''That I am.'' He'd underlined this one.

Alexis smiled, then grabbed a pew Bible, found the passage for the day and handed it over to James. She then opened her own Bible to the required place, determined to concentrate on the sermon.

After a moment she felt a brush along her arm. James's arm along the pew back brought his fingertips against her skin in a featherlight touch. It was probably nothing more than an accidental connection, but nevertheless she had no desire to break the tenuous link. She didn't move.

Unexpectedly, she thought James listened carefully to the sermon. Perhaps in spite of himself? He secretly anticipated boredom, she suspected, but the couple of times she glanced at him, his attention was riveted on the minister. Pastor Dan caught James's attention early on by describing most of the folks who became Jesus's disciples as being very ordinary men. He used humor in his delivery, too, and James laughed along with the others.

Lord, Your word says faith comes by hearing, and hearing by the Word. Please open James's hearing and heart to truly grasp Your love for him and his son. Help him to understand and accept the enormous gift of Your love…what that means to his life.

Afterwards, as the congregation filed out, an old customer of James's engaged him in a lively discussion of lake conditions. He seemed so at ease in the man's company, Alexis had no heart to hurry him. By the time he broke away, a good bit of the parking lot had emptied.

Alexis stood by her car, watching Cliff chase around the asphalt with a younger boy.

"Sorry," James said as he appeared by her side. "Set to go?"

"Yes, I'm ready. We'll be the last there if we don't move along." She reached for her door handle.

James stepped away, half turned toward his truck, which was parked at the edge of the lot. "There's no need to drive two vehicles," he tossed over his shoulder. "Let's take the truck."

She eyed his truck, recalling her struggle to climb into it with grace. "Um, you drove last time," she said in an effort at diplomacy. "Why don't we take my car this time?"

"Believe me. It'll be better if we take my truck," he insisted. "Got fishing equipment in the truck bed. You don't have room in your car for it."

Of course. How foolish of her to forget.

Alexis sighed and glanced down at her dress and heels. She'd packed jeans, a T-shirt and sneakers for the picnic. She should have changed in the church women's room, but she'd thought it better to wait and change at the Bender farmhouse.

"I have a cooler in my trunk," she told him. "Perhaps I should drive, too."

"That's silly. Stay put," he commanded. "I'll be right back."

Alexis gave in and watched him stride away, calling for Cliff as he went. She grabbed the canvas bag that held her clothes. When he pulled his vehicle alongside hers, he dropped to the asphalt and held out his hand for her keys. She handed them over without protest. Letting a man handle that heavy, bulky cooler was all right with her.

"When are we going to eat, Miss Richmond?" Cliff asked, hanging half out of the window as she approached the truck's passenger side.

"Very soon, Cliff," she said, eyeing the distance between the ground and the truck floor. Maybe she could make that high step without a struggle this time.

"But when?"

She handed her bag to Cliff and gathered her skirt in one hand. "I expect they'll have food laid out by the time we arrive."

The cooler landed in the truck bed with a rattle. She placed the ball of one foot on the floor of the cab— then felt two strong hands circle her waist.

"Here you go," James said close to her ear, and lifted her. His breath against her neck sent a dancing sensation down her bare arms. She almost turned her head. Almost, but not quite.

She heard James take a sudden lungful of air, and fleetingly wondered if he liked her scent. She landed on the seat speculating on what might have happened if Cliff weren't watching.

Now, where would that get her except nowhere? she mentally scolded herself. Yet she couldn't deny she'd felt a sudden rush of anticipation.

"What did you bring?" Cliff wanted to know as he scooted to the middle of the bench seat to make room for her.

"Yeah, Teacher," James asked as he climbed into the driver's seat. "What did you bring good to eat?"

"Didn't anyone ever teach the two of you that not everything can be instant gratification? That waiting for the proper time on something can be a good thing?"

"But we already waited all morning," Cliff said.

"And I skipped breakfast," James added.

"Are you one of those men who pay little attention to time, then want to eat the moment you think of it, no matter when that is?"

"I guess so. Are you one of those women who get bent out of shape if meals aren't on the dot?"

"Well, no… Um, sometimes," she admitted.

"Uh-huh." He flashed her a grin. "Admit it. You're not always so rigid. So what did you bring?"

"Deviled eggs and a triple chocolate cake."

James grinned wider and gave her a wink. "Sounds like we need to boogie on down the road, doesn't it, son?"

"Uh-huh. I'm hungry."

She let a chuckle escape her and met James's gaze. It flickered with heat. Then, as he put the truck into gear, James yanked his attention back to the road.

They turned off on a gravel road, and then a dirt lane. Alexis bounced like a ball as the truck did battle with the ruts. The third time Cliff ricocheted off her shoulder, she wriggled around until she could place an arm around his shoulders. It gave them both something of an anchor.

"Now I see why you wanted to drive. I'm grateful

we didn't bring my car,'' she muttered. ''Thank you, James.''

His glance took in her earnest remark. ''You bet. Some of these old roads haven't been improved in a dog's age. They need to be graded.''

By the time they arrived, two tables sat in the yard, already covered with food. They parked next to three other vehicles, and Alexis glanced around as she slid out.

The old cottage farmhouse had a front porch that would offer welcome shade on a hot summer day and dreamy reflections of a long dusk. The farm road led to a weathered barn behind it. Nothing about the place had been modernized except the tightly strung fence that corralled a few head of cattle.

James offered to take care of her cooler while she changed, and Alexis gratefully thanked him.

''Better hurry, folks,'' Caroline Bender, their hostess, called. In her middle years and rather serious, Caroline and her husband Fitz were the Bible Study leaders. ''Everything's ready.''

Tina, from the Pancake House, came forward. Surprised to see her, Alexis glanced around to see who Tina had come with. Perhaps Caroline had invited her?

''Here, I'll take that J.D.,'' Tina said, offering a shy smile. She wore her hair in two braids, which made her appear about twelve. ''All the guys are over there.'' She smiled more broadly at Cliff. ''Hiya, Cliff. You can help me round up the other kids. We're about to have our blessing prayer.''

"I asked Tina to come out to help entertain the kids for the afternoon," Caroline whispered as she led Alexis into the old house. "Some of these youngsters need some corralling."

"Tell me about it," Alexis murmured.

Caroline merely chuckled. "Knew I didn't need to. I knew you, for one, would appreciate joining the adults circle."

In the bedroom, Alexis scrambled to change. Outside the window, she heard Tina introduce Cliff to another child. "This is my cousin, Robby. You two both like video games."

The tone for the afternoon was set. Under Tina's scope, the kids spread out from the adults with games of their own. Cliff, too. He took a shine to Tina, Alexis noted. Whenever Alexis glanced their way she discovered Cliff close to the young woman.

The adults, after clearing away the remains of the meal, talked about the Bible Study they wanted to delve into next. Alexis was pleased when a couple of men invited James to join them on a regular basis.

The surprise came when he didn't immediately turn it down. "I might just do that," he said.

The fishing rods never left the truck bed. James seemed content to sit with the dozen or so adults while the discussion went from town politics to the current economy to family problems. He was especially attentive when one of the couples talked of their efforts to keep their teens in the right crowd.

"The church youth group helps," Sam Winters remarked. "We've some good kids there."

"Yeah, we do," Dean Connor said. "But the way the town's growing, it isn't the same as when we were kids."

"There's no guarantee a kid won't go down the wrong path no matter what you do as a parent," Caroline said. "We gave up a mountain of prayer for Denny when he was a teen. Haven't quit praying, either, especially since he's in St. Louis now. Big city temptations and all...." She turned to James, pursing her mouth. "J.D., you remember the time you and Denny played hooky from school three days in a row to go fishing?"

"Sure do," James answered with a chuckle. "When you and my mom found out, Denny and I were in a heap of trouble. My dad gave me a whale of a walloping. We were only about twelve, though. Not teens."

Alexis listened without comment. So that's where he learned his disciplining tactics. She wondered how often James had endured that kind of corporal punishment.

"True." Caroline nodded. "I made Denny do some community service down at Dr. Sherman's office for it. And he had to do an extra report for school that took him days to write. That sure cured him of playing hooky."

"That you know about, anyway," James said, giving his hostess a cheeky grin.

"Don't tell me about it now, you rascal," Caroline replied. "I'd only want to ground you, and you're far beyond that."

Alexis, sitting across the circle from James, watched his face. Getting caught hadn't prevented *him* from playing hooky. Her teacher's intuition told her so.

What had he done when he should have been in school? Where had he gone? In her experience, a youngster who ditched school often was an unhappy child.

Something unidentifiable flickered in his eyes, but then was quickly hidden. He nodded and grinned in answer to Caroline's comments, but said nothing more. The conversation went in another direction.

Toward evening, the crowd thinned, and some of their company headed back to attend an evening service. Alexis raised a brow in question at James.

"We'd better get going, too." He glanced around for Cliff. "Where did Cliff get to?"

"He's with Tina and Robby," Caroline told them. "I think they're down by the creek."

"I'll go look for them," Alexis offered, and quickly rose from her lawn chair.

James fell into step beside her. As they strolled down the slope toward the creek, the chatter of voices melted away.

A strip of trees loomed ahead. The land became more uneven. The path was clear enough to indicate frequent use, yet Alexis found she needed to pay attention to her footing over the rocks and tree roots. James slid a hand under her elbow. His strength felt comforting as he guided her. Through the trees, she heard the sudden gurgle of water.

"You didn't fish," she mentioned.

He seemed genuinely surprised by her observation. "Never got around to it."

"I thought fishing was your favorite hobby."

"It is. But Cliff was happy without it, and I didn't want to be rude to the others or anything. Actually, I like fishing in the early morning or just at dusk. When it's quiet and still."

"You mean alone."

"Often as I can."

"You are a quiet man sometimes, aren't you, James? Self-contained."

He shot a gaze across the landscape. "Yeah, I suppose I am."

They reached the stream and paused to gaze at the small opening in the trees; the shallow water ran with a slow current. Along the bank a polished tree stump gave evidence of the many bodies that had rested there. Moss clung to the earth beneath it. A few yards down, several large flat rocks also appeared as though they had hosted their share of fishermen.

"This is a peaceful place," Alexis said. She moved to one of the stone seats and sank down. "Rather isolated, though."

"Yep." James lifted his boot to the rock beside her, then leaned on his upraised knee. "But not nearly as isolated as in the twenties, when the house and barn was built. Nobody has kept this place up steadily since the sixties. Caroline never wanted to live out here full time."

"You didn't mention that you knew the Benders when I invited you," Alexis said.

"Didn't think that much about it. Caroline is a distant cousin of my mom's. They were friends, though mom was older by a dozen years or so."

"Ah. So you know this place well. Is this where you and Denny came fishing?"

"Sometimes."

"When you played hooky?"

"Nah." His mouth curved in memory as he stared out at the stream. "This was too easy. We had our own secret place."

"Do you still visit your secret place?"

"Haven't for a long time. Usually too busy with the shop. When I do have time to fish, though, I have a couple of favorite spots on the lake." James's voice softened. "A couple of coves that aren't visited much."

"Where it's quiet and still," she guessed.

"Mm…"

"You're a man who likes your solitude, too."

It was a statement. Would that always be true? Would James always be someone who preferred his own company Did he foresee a time when he could look forward to being alone after Cliff was grown?

"Suppose that's true," he admitted, though a tad reluctantly.

"You lose that when you have a family," she murmured. That might loom as potential trouble for Cliff. Or for anyone who might fall in love with James.

"Does it bother you much? Living with someone…Cliff always around now?"

"I'm getting used to it. He's settling in more. He's finally talking about his mother some. Guess that's good."

"Yes, I'd say that's a very good sign that he's handling things better." She couldn't help herself—her teacher's hat seemed to just settle on her head as she said, "Adjustments aren't always easy, but they're especially hard for a child who's lost a parent. The two of you learning to live together again takes fresh thinking."

His brow lowered a fraction. "Appears I'm doing a lot of that these days."

"Does that scare you?"

"Teach—" he tipped his head and looked at her directly "—it scares the living stuffing out of me. But…"

"But?"

"But I don't think I can go back." He eased off the rock and stared down into her face. "I can't undo anything in the past, so what's the point? Don't know that I'd want to if I could. That scares me, too. You know what I mean?"

"Yes, I think I do." Alexis brushed her hair behind her ear, wondering about her own need to implement a new thought pattern. "I guess something new—"

He bent without warning and slid his palm against her cheek, his fingers splaying through her hair.

"Something beyond my norm," he muttered, a rascally glint shimmering in his brown eyes.

His mouth came down on hers, warm and welcome, and more exciting than any kiss she'd experienced. Her skin prickled. Her heart quickened.

Whoa, here… she told herself before all thought left her. If she wasn't careful, she'd find herself racing higher than the treetops. *Slow down….*

She couldn't.

She parted her lips in response. Instantly, his mouth gently spread wider over hers, and the thought darted through her mind that her racing heart was already out of control. Her whole body stretched upward towards him, her fingers spread out on his shoulders. In response, his thumb stroked the line of her jaw, giving her the impression that the skin just beneath was starving for his touch.

A boyish *whoop* pierced their quiet. Alexis heard laughter and splashing.

James pulled away, his breathing rapid. His eyes looked like dark melted chocolate. Then his lids dropped, shuttering his emotions. "Alexis, I—"

"Boys, come on out of the water now." Tina's young female voice intruded. By the sound of things, her gentle bid went unheeded. "Boys, please! Your parents will skin me if you're all wet with no dry clothes to change into."

"I think it's probably too late," James muttered, chuckling. "Bets are on that they're already soaked."

As Tina came into view, James strode downstream, shouting a deep command to the boys. Alexis listened as the boys called out, full of youthful exhilaration.

Shakily, she rose from her stone seat, working to compose her expression before Tina caught up to her.

What had James been about to say?

She asked herself that question again on the long drive home.

And once again before falling asleep, alone in her tiny apartment.

Chapter Seven

"How about meeting over lunch today?" Lori suggested on Tuesday morning. This was their second try at arranging a meeting. They hurried through the rain to enter the school building as a clap of thunder rolled past. "We can get our dates set for our field trips and line up the bus. I want to take a trip to the dam, too."

"Yeah, that would be a good trip to take. I think I can manage Tuesday morning. Let me check with Kathy."

They stopped at the office. Alexis hoped to grab the copy machine before the morning started, but Elizabeth, the office secretary, was there before her. Alexis shuffled through her messages. One was a request from a parent for a meeting this week, and one was from the superintendent.

"Oh," Lori muttered, frowning over her own identical message. "Fisher is a real pain about this reorganization plan. I hope he doesn't stick us with a principal from out of the county. And he's holding this meeting over at Lawson?''

Elizabeth gave them a hard stare. Lori motioned Alexis to move on down the hall.

"Wonder if he'd notice if I skipped it this time," Lori said. Lawson, the next town over, added another thirty minutes' driving time to their meeting. "Thursday is already a long day for me, and Steven gripes all through dinner when I have to go out again for an evening meeting."

"Fisher has been pretty adamant about support from everyone," Alexis remarked. She sympathized with Lori's plight, knowing her friend also juggled taking care of an elderly grandmother.

Alexis stuffed the message into her purse. Her Bible Study was on Thursday evenings. She hated missing that.

Lori sighed as they turned down the hall toward their classrooms. Around them, kids began to swirl through the corridor. "Yeah, he takes it personally if we don't show up."

"I know," Alexis said as she neatly sidestepped an oncoming sixth grader. "He is still suspicious of me, since my original teaching certification came from another state. The fact that I have my Masters from Missouri doesn't seem to mitigate his opinion that I'm a foreign invader into his territory."

Lori chuckled, showing her dimples. They paused at the corner that branched from the main hall.

"I think he's planning to move into state politics," Lori said with a conspiratorial wink. "He won't be happy until he's running more than the school system." They looked at each other a minute, trying to picture their esteemed leader in state politics. Lori shuddered, then burst out laughing. "Oh, well. Guess we'll have to suffer through. By the way, did you and J.D. have a nice weekend?"

"Sunday's picnic was lovely," Alexis replied. She tried hard to convey all the pleasantries of the day and not think about the kiss she'd shared with J.D. She had been trying not to think of J.D. period. She glanced down the hall, looking for her students.

"That's what I heard from Caroline."

That brought her attention around. "You know Caroline Bender?"

"Mmm-hmm… Used to date their son Denny."

"Mercy. I think I've dropped into the colossal, premier town circle." Alexis shook her head in amazement. "It's something like Alice's rabbit hole to an outsider. You weren't a part of their playing hooky days, were you?"

"Nope. But I wanted to be." Lori's mischievous dimples disappeared as she lowered her voice. "Alexis, I'm really glad for J.D. that you're giving him some long-needed extra attention, and God knows Cliff needs it. But I'd be careful, if I were you, around Fisher."

"What do you mean?"

"I mean I wouldn't mention personal issues around our esteemed superintendent. And anything you say around Elizabeth is pipelined right to him. Fisher has been on a tear…um, he doesn't think teachers should fraternize with the civilians, if you know what I mean.''

''Not really.'' Alexis feared it might be a tad too late. ''What do you mean?''

Lori paused at her classroom door and glanced about them to see who might be nearby.

''Well...there was a ten-alarm scandal a few years back when a high school teacher was caught in a compromising situation with a student, and the parent...''

Lori paused, remaining quiet as three students passed them.

''What happened?'' Alexis asked.

''It was an awful mess, and even though I think the teacher innocent of harmful intent, it looked very bad and...she was fired. Mr. Fisher has been more than a little paranoid about our district reputation since then. He doesn't want even a hint of impropriety to smudge his record.''

''Yes, I can see why.'' Trust in teachers held the same level of social expectation as that in other professionals: doctors, lawyers, ministers. They needed to be above reproach. It could be a mistake for her to form a friendship outside the teacher-student relationship, no matter how much the child may need help.

Yet how could she hold back her help toward a child like Cliff? Knowing that she could make a difference? Knowing James welcomed it?

''Thanks, Lori. I'll see you later.''

Alexis turned in to her own classroom with yellow ''Caution'' signals rattling around her head. Her friend meant only to help her, and Lori's caution was an honest one. Yet that didn't necessarily cover a relationship between two single adults, did it? As long as they were free of other entanglements? She and James...

Once again her attempt to block thoughts of James was failing miserably.

Memories of their kiss still had the power to send her heart into a triple spin. Yet it was only a single kiss, she reasoned. She could put it away, pretend it never happened, while she still had time to distance herself from a potential problem. Perhaps she should take giant steps back from James...er, the Sullivan family.

Could she?

Cliff bounced into the room then, just ahead of the bus students streaming in. He plopped a note on her desk before going to his seat.

Seeing it, her knees went weak. The oddest tingling shot up the side of her neck. She slid her hand against the sensation, rubbing just where James's palm had lain yesterday.

The bell rang, jerking her back to the present. She whipped the note out of sight into her top desk drawer, to read later. Putting aside her personal thoughts, Alexis concentrated her attention on her classroom, reminding herself of one very important point.

All of these kids needed her.

At recess, she hurried to the teacher's lunchroom to grab a cup of coffee and a muffin. She'd forgone breakfast. James's note practically burned a hole in her pocket, but while last week she wouldn't have hesitated to read it in front of other teachers or office staff, now she chose to save it for a private moment.

She was thankful that Lori had other duties during her recess break. Alexis didn't feel socially bound to remain in the lounge, so she made an excuse of needing to work and carried her goodies back to her room. She settled down at her desk and opened the note.

"Cliff said you mentioned in class that your sewing machine is not working correctly," James wrote. "I'll be at the shop till five. Bring it by this afternoon and I'll see what's wrong with it."

Now, that was a nice offer. She couldn't help the smile that spread across her face. To her knowledge there was no one in town who did sewing machine repair. And her curiosity was peaked to see James's shop. She'd never been inside Sullivan's Repair.

Well, why not? Her machine was an old one she'd inherited from her aunt Nancy, not one of the new computerized variety. There weren't too many people offering service on the old machines anymore. Surely no one could fault her for getting her sewing machine repaired?

Then she remembered. It was her turn to monitor after school detention.

She'd have to rush if she wanted to make it to the shop before closing time.

Sullivan's Repair sat in an old strip mall of six shops on Main Street—the old main drag of Sunny Creek. She found a parking spot in front of it, marked on a slant. She'd pushed her time to the limit, racing home after school to gather up her machine. The clock hanging in the insurance office next door read four fifty-five.

She slammed her door and hefted her twenty-year-old portable sewing machine across the sidewalk.

"Here, why didn't you let me haul that for you?" James asked, coming forward to take it from her as she shouldered her way through the door.

"Thanks. I didn't have any trouble with it," she said, noticing another man leaning against the front counter. "Though I have to admit it is a bit heavy."

The man, who was in his early fifties, nodded a friendly greeting. His attitude was nonchalant, but he held himself as one used to command. He wore jeans and a sport shirt, but Alexis guessed his clothing wasn't out of a discount store. Neither were his expensive leather shoes.

"Hi, Miss Richmond," Cliff said. "I'm helping my dad with counting the catalogs he's got behind the counter. I'm throwing out all the old ones."

"That's an excellent task, Cliff." She ruffled his hair, eliciting a pleased glance. She gazed around at the neat shelves, offering canoe paddles, life vests, propellers, and a sectioned line of engine parts. Large pictures of well-known boat designs stared at her from the wall behind the counter. Lower still was another sectioned bin of more engine parts.

"Look at this, Miss Richmond," Cliff urged, pointing to a glossy flyer that featured a speedboat sluicing through the water. "See this boat? I'm gonna get a boat like this someday. It's the fastest kind on the lake, isn't it, Dad?''

''That depends on the engine, son,'' James pointed out.

He turned to the other man, evidently finishing his transaction. ''I can be out to your place on Friday afternoon to pull that motor, Galen. It probably needs a good clean. Will you be there to let me into your boathouse?''

''I'll see that I am, J.D. And I appreciate your immediate attention to it. I'd like my boat in good running order before the month is out. I have guests coming to stay.''

''Sure thing, Galen.''

The customer left, and James turned his attention her way. ''That guy owns a summer place out on the main channel. He's been a great customer. Don't know why, but he sends me business from all over the lake.''

Alexis tipped her head and studied James. He'd been entirely easy with his customer when discussing business. There was nothing awkward about their interchange.

''He must believe you deserve his patronage, James,'' she said slowly.

Actually, James had a great way with customers. She'd heard as much from Caroline, and now had observed it for herself. Didn't he understand his own strengths? ''If you didn't do a good job with your business and offer the best of services, he wouldn't bother. Men with that kind of power don't.''

James's brow lowered in puzzlement. "That kind of power?"

"That's Galen Stallings, isn't it?"

"Uh-huh." He lifted her sewing machine and carried it through to his back room. "That's his name."

"I've read about him. He's the CEO of Challenge Technologies," she said, following him.

"So?"

"So? Don't you read the financial reports? His company makes hospital technical equipment, but they also thrive on top-notch service. He's been featured in leading business magazines for years."

"No kidding?" he said, setting the machine on a work counter and taking off the lid. "Well, I knew the man had money. His place on the lake spreads out over twenty acres."

"You don't seem impressed."

"Guess not." He bent to peer into the inner workings. "To me, he's just Galen. We do a bit of fishing together now and then. How long has it been since you've cleaned this machine?"

He'd changed subjects in one breath.

"It had an overhaul about two years ago, I think," she answered, then pursued her runaway thought. "James, doesn't it interest you that this man can boost your business?"

"Got enough business. More than I can handle in boating seasons." Fingering the presser foot, he said, "Tell me what's amiss with it."

"The tension is way off and doesn't want to hold—

Do you have enough customers to expand your shop?''

He turned to rummage through a cardboard box, then pulled out what appeared to be the remnants of an old shirt. ''Sometimes think about it, but so far it's more trouble than it's worth.''

He tore a chunk of fabric from the shirttail.

''But if you had help you could gain more time for yourself and not have to put in so many hours.''

He turned, and his eyes held exasperation, his mouth hardened. ''Yeah, but I can't carry anyone through the winter, Alexis, and I can't pay top wages either. Anyone who wants a job can go into the new stores out on the highway and make better pay. Benefits, too.''

He bent to plug in the sewing machine.

She bit her lip against saying more, but couldn't help herself. She pushed. ''Surely there's a way to make it work. Have you tried?''

''Not recently,'' he snapped, and tipped his head toward where Cliff shuffled through catalogs. ''And I'm not in much of a position to do any expanding in the near future, either.''

The phone rang, and he snatched up the extension on the wall beside the workbench. He clapped the receiver against his ear, nearly snapping into the phone, ''Sullivan's Repair.''

She'd made him angry, and regret hammered through her. Who was she to give business advice to anyone? She knew nothing at all about running a business. She didn't know James well enough to be lecturing him on how to run his. She'd already over-stepped her boundaries in her advice about his son.

She'd been presumptuous. How could she have al-lowed her thoughts to pop out like that? Usually she was more thoughtful with her friends, and certainly didn't think of herself as an interfering type of person.

Perhaps it was a good time for her to leave.

Sorry, she mouthed at him, knowing her embar-rassment showed in the color in her cheeks. Motioning that she was going, she turned.

He hooked his long fingers around her wrist, hold-ing her in place while he finished his conversation.

"Yeah, Harry, I'll be there on time. Mrs. Shoe-maker, my neighbor, agreed to sit with Cliff. I just have to get out by nine or so."

James hung up, then stared at her.

Alexis wanted to apologize for her rudeness, but she couldn't seem to get the words out. Her mouth felt dry.

Slowly, James released her wrist. And slowly, Alexis realized she didn't want him to let go—yet she didn't have the courage to turn her hand into his.

The longer she waited to say something, the harder it would be.

"I'm sorry, James," she said on a rush. Ashamed as she felt, she didn't allow her gaze to waver. "I shouldn't have stuck my nose into your operation. You didn't ask for my opinion, and I know nothing at all about business."

"I know." His mouth curved with sudden humor.

"Yeah, well..." He didn't have to say it with so much amusement.

"The Main Street Business Association meets tonight," James said, explaining his phone call.

"Oh."

"I'll be through shortly after nine."

"That's good, I suppose. You'll be home in time to tuck Cliff into bed."

Cliff was singing a pop song in the front of the store, his off-key tone climbing higher on the scale as he went.

"You mentioned that mushy stuff before. But I think Cliff is a little old to be tucked into bed," he said with a shade of disgust.

"You might think so, James." This was a subject she did know about, and she warmed to it. "But nine isn't all that grown up. And he has only you now. I don't think a child ever outgrows the need for a parent's affection, and he's going to need to hear that you love him every day for a very long time."

His eyes narrowed. "You really think Cliff feels neglected?"

"Sometimes."

"And he'd like it? Tucking him in bed?"

"Why don't you try it and see?"

"All right."

She nodded. "Well, I have to go."

She backed away a few steps toward the door. He followed. "You need to take care of closing up and everything. And I apologize again for assuming...well, you know. Thanks for...uh...thanks."

"It's nothing. I'll call you when I'm finished."

"You will?"

"With your sewing machine."

"Oh. That's good."

She could hardly wait to receive his call—not that she'd ever admit it out loud.

Chapter Eight

$\varsigma\!\!\sim\!\!\bullet$

Call her he did, but it had nothing to do with her sewing machine. Alexis didn't admit even to herself that she was as happy as a kid at Christmas just to hear his voice. She simply felt it.

"I don't know if it made a difference or not, but I got home just in time to say good-night to Cliff before he went off to sleep," James said, his enthusiasm radiating past his hello. "Tucked him in like you suggested. He settled down pretty good."

Alexis glanced at her bedside clock—ten past ten. She'd been reading papers, propped up in bed, since nine-thirty. She held a sheaf of papers closer against her chest.

"Oh, that's good, James. You're making real progress with him."

Secretly, she was more than thrilled that her suggestion had paid off. There was nothing like a little success to foster more effort. "Cliff will respond more positively, believe me. Maybe it won't be evident yet for a while, but eventually.''

"I sure hope so.'' A note of doubt crept into his tone. "Didn't imagine I'd be…well, a nine-year-old son…''

"Cliff isn't the normal nine-year-old, now, is he?'' she said. "Special children need special attention. In fact, every child deserves the best from a parent.'' Then, realizing she was spouting her teacher's philosophy, with implied criticism, she bit her lip. "Um, besides, you haven't been raising him until lately.''

"You got that right. And I'm discovering that making up for those lost years is no easy feat.''

He didn't sound as though he'd taken offense from her pushy statements. She hoped he'd forgotten her earlier brashness, too.

His voice deepened with regret. "Wish I'd had more sense when he was little. I was stretched tighter that a bowstring trying to earn a living, and too young, and Melanie—'' He broke off, his indrawn breath conveying a mix of emotions.

Alexis wondered what he'd been about to say concerning Cliff's mother. For the first time she wondered why James and Melanie Sullivan hadn't made their marriage work. That they'd been very young when they married, she knew from Lori. And she'd learned a little about Cliff's life before returning to live with his dad from Cliff himself.

She suspected Melanie hadn't been too involved with her son's needs, at least for the past year or so.

Had Melanie treated James with the same self-centered indifference?

James spoke again. "Seems I have a lot to learn."

"You'll do it, James," she said, intent on encouraging him. "If you want it."

"Yeah. Well." His tone went a little formal. "Thanks for your help, Miss Richmond. See you around school sometime."

For some reason his indifferent end to their conversation stung.

Alexis and Lori traveled together for the district-wide meeting at Lawson.

"Don't know why we have to be here," Lori groused as she parked. "We need this redistricting, and it should go through without much trouble."

"I'm assuming Mr. Fisher wants a show of support for his plan," Alexis said. "I hear there's a move from the opposition to cut the districts into smaller pieces than Fisher is happy with."

"Yeah. In my opinion, Mr. Fisher has a hard time sharing control," Lori said, lowering her voice as they took their seats.

Lori and Alexis sat through a long evening of endless discussion and debate with dutiful attention, and then started home, both in yawns.

"Coffee," Lori muttered as she started her car. "I need a cup of coffee to keep awake, or we may not get home in one piece."

"Me, too," Alexis agreed, then as they pulled onto

the highway, suggested, "We can stop at that diner up ahead and get it to go."

"Great," Lori said as she pulled into the parking lot, then dug into her purse for her cell phone. "Tell you what. You go in for it while I call my honey. Steven will be in a tizzy of worry if I don't let him know where I am and when I'll be home."

Alexis went inside and ordered the coffee at the counter.

"It'll take just a minute, hon," said the middle-aged waitress. "Just made a fresh pot and it's almost done. Have a seat if you wanta."

"That's fine. I'll be right here."

While she waited, she counted out the exact change she'd need. Two men rose from a booth and came forward to stand near the cash register, waiting for the waitress's return. They talked in low tones, to which she did not pay the slightest heed—until one man addressed the other as Galen, saying, "I'll hop right on it and file tomorrow. Then I'll send you copies."

"Do that. And send two sets, one to my city office and one to my lake address. I want the plans approved by next week."

Galen Stallings?

Alexis glanced over her shoulder just as the waitress arrived with two foam cups. Galen Stallings caught her stare. She had no idea if he recognized her from seeing her in Sullivan's Repair, but he gave a slight nod. He seemed to acknowledge an acquaintance.

The other man didn't notice.

She plunked the money on the counter, grabbed

some napkins from the container sitting next to the register and hurried out.

"Lovely," Lori said as she accepted her cup and turned on her motor. "Now talk to me. Keep me alert. But I don't want to hear another word about county plans tonight."

"Okay." Alexis chuckled and buckled her seat belt. "Do you know who Galen Stallings is?"

"Sure. Pretty much everyone in town knows Galen." Lori sipped from her cup, then pulled out onto the highway. "He has a large place on the lake. Entertains all summer. Why?"

"Nothing much. I saw him at James's shop the other day."

"Galen's popular," Lori said, placing her cup in the holder. "He likes to support the local merchants and businesses, and spends his money freely. He's been good to Sunny Creek. You saw him in J.D.'s shop? Wow, he's down early this year."

"Is he?" Alexis shrugged. "Well, I just saw him in the diner back there with another guy."

"Oh, really? Who was the other guy?"

"Don't know, I have never seen him before. Short, about thirty, sandy hair."

"Uh-oh. That sounds like Keith Baldwin. A local who went to work for Galen up in Chicago. Wonder what the two of them are up to...."

"Who can say?"

Lori turned on her high beams and slowed as they hit a long stretch of roller-coaster-like, tree-dense road. "So...you met Galen at J.D.'s shop, huh?"

"Uh-huh. James is repairing my sewing machine."

"That's very in-ter-est-ing," Lori said, stretching the word out. "J.D. has never offered to repair anything for me."

"Now, Lori, don't read into it."

"Not me, girl. *I* wouldn't do such a thing. Just because he's one of Sunny Creek's best-looking men ever. I know half a dozen women… Oh, never mind."

"You're too much," Alexis said, chuckling. "And I thought you didn't approve of a teacher dating a parent. Afraid of what Mr. Fisher would say?"

"Well, there's that. On the other hand, it's about time J.D. showed real interest in someone again. I think you might be very good for J.D. After all, didn't you say he went to church, even?"

"Yes, actually. We— Um, James thinks it would be good for Cliff."

"See? You are a good influence. Just don't let Fisher know anything until the school year is over."

"Well, there's nothing to know."

Nothing but a kiss between them.

Alexis pushed the seam along under the presser foot, hoping to finish the vest before leaving for her Thursday evening Bible Study. She marveled at how much better the thread tension held since James returned her sewing machine to her. The man did have a way with machines.

She carefully turned the point and clipped the threads. That was all she'd do for now, she decided.

She had agreed to sew eight vests, and this was number six.

The May concert, only ten days away, involved the fifth and sixth graders' choir, and a handful of band members. Two other teachers and one mother had set up a sewing crew in the teachers lounge, agreeing that two hours after school for several days should do the job. Only, today they had run way overtime. Alexis shared the sewing with the young mother, Judy Wilson.

Why she'd agreed to help sew, Alexis didn't have a clue. She wasn't even involved in the choir, nor were any of her students. At the time, she supposed, she thought she'd have lots of time on her hands because she'd just broken up with Ron.

She chuckled at herself. Her attachment to Ron seemed like a lifetime ago, and her thoughts seldom dwelled on him these days. That in itself was a revelation. That she hadn't truly loved him was a thought growing in her consciousness like crabgrass. Not only that, Ron hadn't really been interested in marriage. Why had she even thought it? He had really been looking for someone who would be a perfect corporate wife, she supposed—someone to fit his life. Well, he hadn't fit nearly enough of the points on her list of desired qualities.

Neither did James Dean Sullivan. Not even close.

"Oh, who cares?" she said aloud, startling even herself. It wasn't likely they'd sustain enough interest in each other to categorize it as a relationship.

So, why couldn't she stop thinking of him?

"What's that, Alexis?" Lori asked, breezing into the teachers lounge on her way home, juggling her purse and a canvas bag of papers. "Aren't you ladies going home tonight?"

"Um, nothing," Alexis muttered. "Just that I don't think there's enough of this black braid to finish the trim on thirty-four vests."

"Oh, no…" Judy exclaimed. "I bought all the braid that store had. I was sure it would be enough."

"Well, I think we'll run short by a couple of yards," Alexis said. "We'll need more."

Lori came over to study the braid. "I bet you'll find it in Sedalia."

"Don't think so," Judy said. "Although the store can reorder it, I think. But even if I called the store, it will take time to get it in—and I don't have any more time this week to run over there."

"I'll look for it in Kansas City when I visit my parents on Saturday," Alexis said. "If Lori will take my after-school detention on Friday."

Lori groaned. "All right. But then you have to help with lining up parents for our field trip over to the dam. I'm having problems."

"It's a deal," Alexis agreed. "But I have to run now. I'm late for my Bible Study."

Twenty minutes later Alexis parked her car alongside a few others in the church lot, then raced into the building. Almost fifteen minutes late. Thursdays stood out as her favorite weeknight. The Bible Study expanded her understanding of God's word and challenged her to greater faith; usually she never let anything interfere with her attendance. She'd missed last week only because of the required school district meeting.

Fitz Bender's baritone hit her ears as soon as she opened the door. Hebrews…

She burst into the classroom they used, apologies for her tardiness on her lips, then stopped cold. Among the usual circle of a dozen people, James sat in one corner, an old Bible draped over his knee.

What was he doing here? She hadn't seen his truck in the parking lot. Then she remembered. She'd invited him. Only, she hadn't really expected him to come.

An uncertain smile tugged at her mouth. In response, a roguish grin spread across James's, his brown-eyed lightning glance a telltale communication for any who caught it.

He'd come because he knew she'd be there.

Alexis blinked, breaking the contact, then flashed a glance around the circle as she wondered who may have noticed. "Sorry to be late, everyone. I didn't mean to disrupt the study."

She took the empty chair opposite James. As quietly as possible, she flipped through her Bible to find the scripture, as Fitz picked up his reading.

"'…without faith it is impossible to please God, because anyone who comes to him must believe that he exists and that he rewards those who earnestly seek him.'"

She tried not to be too aware of James. Yet his very

presence made her aware—he was masculine and good looking, and he made her tempted to flirt shamelessly.

The very thought brought a heat to her cheeks. She buried her gaze in Hebrews, barely following Fitz's comments.

Except for the quick delivery of her repaired sewing machine, a five-minute exchange accomplished in the company of Lori and two other teachers, Alexis hadn't seen James lately. She'd had little to report to him on Cliff's behavior, and had written only one note to go home. James's reply had been short and to the point. Nothing more than what any parent might reply.

Alexis peeked up from her open Bible. She secretly studied his face. His wide mouth lay relaxed, his clean-shaven chin slightly thrust out in concentration. His dark lashes fanned out against his cheek, as he focused his attention on the scripture.

She silently let her breath out and returned her gaze to the open book. Three minutes later, her lashes drifted up again. And again…

Caroline finally tipped her head, giving her a quizzical gaze.

Alexis smiled, trying to cover her guilt. How could she say that she simply couldn't help herself? She had to look at James. What was wrong in trying to assess how things were with him? Trying to grasp the progress between him and his son. How his week was going? How the scripture affected him? What he thought of the commentary? Or admitting she found him so attractive that he tumbled everything else out of her mind when he was around…that something about him drew her…that she'd missed him this week.

And that those rushing thoughts scrambled her emotions into confusion. How could she? She still barely knew James, and after the end of the school year, what would bring them together? They had so little in common.

Yet, under Caroline's open curiosity, she thought it better to concentrate on the study. Usually she found it vitally interesting.

This evening it felt like pulling horses through a knothole to keep her attention there.

At a few minutes past nine, Fitz concluded the evening with prayer. As was their custom, they gathered in a circle and clasped hands. Also, as usual, a few prayer needs were voiced.

Alexis sent up her requests silently. *Lord, I know James is here for his own reasons, but help him to learn more of You…draw him nearer, let him open his heart to You completely. May Your word take root and grow in his heart and mind. And Lord, please guide me…let me hear Your wisdom…don't let me make another mistake in judgment.*

She'd dated a boy in college who only liked her because she was smart and could help him with his studies. When her use to him was over, so was the romance. Several boyfriends followed, but she discarded them easily when she found they had a fault she didn't like. Ron had seemed stable, handsome and ambitious. But as time went on, his ambition to climb the corporate ladder took over his life. He thought of little else. And Alexis found his lack of attention had ruined their romance.

She hadn't really loved Ron, she supposed. Not enough to follow him to Dallas. She'd been in love with the idea of marriage.

As they walked out and dispersed with the usual small talk, Alexis found Caroline beside her.

"You're usually on time, Alexis. Anything the matter?"

"Not at all." She glanced at James, in earnest conversation with Fitz. His face fell into sober lines as he talked. She wondered what they discussed.

"It's good to see J.D. here tonight," Caroline murmured, glancing to where her husband and James were talking. "I think you must have had something to do with that."

"I wish I could say I did, Caroline, but I didn't know he was coming." Surprised at how much she did wish it threaded through her mulling thoughts. "I did ask him once. He said he had too much to do."

"Whatever the reason, I'm very glad. His mother would be so happy to know he is interesting in God's word."

Various members of the group called good-night as they drove away. James was leaning against Fitz and Caroline's car, lost to those around him.

Beyond the parking light, the night throbbed with spring sounds. A nearby open door shared TV noise. Though it was a school night, Alexis noticed a child whizzing by on his bicycle. She called her own good-night. James didn't notice.

She drove home thinking of the papers she still had to correct and a lesson plan she had to take care of. She pulled into the drive of the house where her apartment was located and climbed out. She gathered her bag of papers, her purse, her Bible, and locked her car.

Then headlights nearly blinded her as a black truck pulled in behind her car. Brakes slammed on. The headlights shut off. The motor went silent…and a tall figure climbed out.

"Alexis."

She held up her hand. "James?"

"Yeah, it's me." He came toward her with a slow, purposeful stride.

"Oh…do you want something?" She set her heavy book bag on her car hood and relaxed against the car. "Need something?"

"Sure do." He stopped in front of her. Her block streetlight stood on the corner, four houses down. Cloud cover gave her no moonlight by which to see his expression.

"What is it?"

"Have to finish something."

"I don't recall—"

He said nothing more. He leaned in and placed his lips on hers, lingering, gently pressing her words into nonexistence. He made no effort to gather her body close to his. Instead, his long fingers threaded through her hair to curve against the back of her head. His thumb stroked her cheek just in front of her ear.

His withdrawal came bit by bit, leaving Alexis tingling all over. He stared at her, only a few inches dividing them. She blinked. Her breath had been stolen....

"Alexis?" James sounded a bit breathless, too.

"Yes?"

"How's your Friday night next week?"

"It's..." *Empty* was the word that came first to mind. Yet that wasn't exactly true. Her life didn't feel empty, but her free time had definitely changed. Up until recently she'd gone up to Kansas City most weekends to spend time with Ron and her parents—but mostly with Ron. Their breakup had changed all that.

She drew a deep breath and said, "It's free."

"Want to see a movie?"

"Sure. What does Cliff want to see?"

"I don't know, but he's spending the night with his new friend, Robby. The boy's mother was kind enough to watch Cliff for me tonight."

"Oh." Her thoughts went spinning. Just the two of them? No mingling crowd from church or school to hide among?

She thought of Lori's recent remarks about Fisher's disapproval of teachers becoming too involved with students. She and James would be on a date, not just sharing church activities. In Fisher's view, she supposed, she'd be stepping over the line.

Yet they already had, hadn't they? With that kiss?

Mentally, she counted several reasons why she should refuse, reasons other than displeasing Fisher. Sexy as she found him, she knew James was unlike her idea of good husband material. After all, he didn't appear good at long-term relationships. They did share their concern for Cliff, however....

Wisdom dictated she refuse—or at least take some time to think seriously about it.

But the kiss they'd just shared was certainly serious enough.

"So, how about it?" His very normal tone instantly smothered her wayward thoughts. "We'll drive over to Sedalia and see what's showing. We can eat Chinese."

She swallowed hard and moistened her lips before answering. "You like Chinese food?"

He tilted his head, a grin shooting across his face. "Yeah. So?"

"I would have thought you strictly a meat-and-potatoes kind of guy," she admitted, responding to his grin.

"Not necessarily. Don't pigeonhole me. So, you want to go or not?"

Well, why not? It was only a movie. She'd need a break by next Friday, and Sedalia was big enough to rattle around in without running into acquaintances. It might be just the thing to lighten up her week.

"Sure," she answered, as casually as possible.

Casual? Who was she kidding? The thought of a real date with James sent her into a tizzy of expectation, and all her mental cautions went out the window. Her decision had nothing to do with what or where they ate dinner, but she added, "I love Chinese food."

"Okay. I'll pick you up about six."

Chapter Nine

The following Friday James closed Sullivan's Repair thirty minutes early, to deliver Cliff and pizza to Robby's house across town. He spent half the drive over lecturing Cliff on how to behave while a guest at his friend's house, all the while wondering when he'd become a stodgy old man.

That didn't last long. As he hurried back home for a quick shower and his second shave of the day, he felt as if he was twenty again, ready to roar on a Friday night. He couldn't recall the last time he'd looked forward to a date with this much excitement.

He couldn't remember a woman who excited him this much—ever.

Keeping in mind that Alexis was a classy lady, he dug through his closet until he found a pair of black dress slacks and a pair of black loafers he hadn't worn in a year.

He spent twenty minutes on spit and shine.

He hauled out the seldom-used iron, and pressed his pants. He pulled out four sport shirts before he found one that wasn't torn, stained or limp with age.

Holding up the blue check he finally decided on, he shook his head. Man, Cliff wasn't the only one who could be a slob. Living alone didn't promote the same kind of neatness at home that he felt so strongly about down at the shop. It was time he sorted through his stuff and threw some of it out, he guessed. He could use some new clothes.

Yes sir, he and Cliff should do some shopping. Especially now, if he and his boy expected to attend church and all. He hadn't felt uncomfortable in his denims, and other worshipers had dressed casually, but it might please Alexis if he wore something nice for Sunday worship.

The idea of pleasing Alexis tickled his grin to spread. Yet, putting that aside, the worship service itself had sparked something new in his thinking. Being there hadn't felt awkward at all. He'd actually been intrigued with the pastor's message. The second Sunday, too. Interested enough to dig out the Bible his mother had given him on his twelfth birthday. He'd found hers, as well, marked and worn by her years of use, while his remained almost brittle with disuse.

His mom's lay by his bedside; he glanced at it as he shoved his legs through the dark pants. Seeing it there almost made him feel she was with him again. His mom had underlined enough passages for him to easily find some of the same scriptures that had brought her comfort. He'd promised himself to read

from it on his own, without prompting from the Bible
Study—though he liked the Thursday evenings well
enough. He'd known some of the group all his life;
Caroline and Fitz had been a part of his growing up.

Mom had prayed for him regularly, that he knew.

He'd been a willful child, right enough, full of pride
and stubbornness. Not unlike Cliff, he supposed. And
he'd suffered enough punishments for it from his father. In spite of all that, his mother's love never wa-
vered. She'd prayed for him her whole life and would
be the first to encourage him to read the scriptures.

Well, he'd do it. After all, if he expected God to
help him with his son, J.D. figured it only right to
learn more about God's son. By his own neglect, his
childhood Bible lessons were all too rare for honest
faith to have taken hold. Now he needed it.

He needed it for his kid. For himself. For whatever
future lay in store....

*Lord, if You're there, I'd appreciate Your help. I
have nothing much to offer You or anyone. Don't
know why I'm so hyped about Alexis. It isn't likely
she'd really fall for a lunkhead like me....*

Lunkhead, and worse. It didn't matter. He'd take as
much of her company as she was willing to give him.
And tonight he didn't have to share her with anyone
else.

He stood, checking everything that went into his
pockets. His pulse rate quickened with anticipation.
Last night after Bible Study, he'd been unable to help
himself in following her home for a good-night kiss.

He'd thought of her every day, for sure. His busy days since that picnic kiss had been too long a gap.

J.D. left his small four-room rental house on the edge of town and drove into the original part of Sunny Creek. Alexis lived in an attic apartment on a street he'd been down dozens of times. Promptly at seven he climbed the wooden outside stairs two at a time. From inside he heard a soft melody—violins, he thought, from a tape or CD. He rapped firmly against her door.

He was very glad he'd taken the extra time to find something nice to wear. When Alexis opened her door, a bit of lace on a pink blouse framed her graceful neck and face. She wore more makeup than usual; her lashes appeared longer and her lips more defined. She looked so good he didn't say a word for one long minute.

"Hi." He finally let his breath out. "You look nice."

She looked nice? Couldn't he think of something better to say than "nice"?

"Thanks." Her smile sent a bubbling through his veins like a kid's fizzy water. There was a light of approval in her gaze when she looked at him, sending his pulse rate even higher. It made him want to grab her around the middle and swing her high.

"So, do you want to come in for a moment?" she asked.

"Sure." He gestured to her. "Unless you're ready?"

"I'm ready. Just let me get a sweater."

He stepped through the door into a small living room, and remained there. Just beyond was the equally small kitchen. The bedroom would be in the back, he surmised. This apartment came furnished, he knew, like a handful of others in this older neighborhood.

He glanced about for her personal touches. Books on the floor beside a two-seater couch. A laptop computer on the scarred coffee table. A bunch of fresh jonquils— he stored a thought away for future reference. She liked fresh flowers.

A candy wrapper, half hidden behind the computer, brought him a grin. She liked coconut candy.

Alexis reappeared with an ivory cardigan sweater over her arm. He waited while she locked her door, then led her down the outside stairway to a four-year-old blue compact car. She cast him a quizzical look.

He shrugged. "I borrowed a loaner from Bill, over on Fifth and Main."

"That is very thoughtful of you, James."

Her compliment swelled his chest, and he opened her door. She slid in with an ease she hadn't felt struggling into his old rattletrap.

For a change, he'd done something right with a woman. Usually, he wasn't much good with them past a surface attraction. An attraction that progressed to a genuine relationship always seemed just beyond his reach. When it came to holding on, he just didn't have it. It hadn't been hard for Melanie to walk away. It hadn't been hard for other women to walk away either.

On the other hand, he hadn't given anyone the chance to stick around since Melanie.

"Was Cliff happy about spending the night with Robby?" Alexis asked.

"Yeah, I think so. I just hope he behaves himself." He walked around to the driver's side, recalling the talking-to he'd given his son about not acting up. "I warned Sara, Robby's mom, that Cliff can be a handful sometimes, but she said after raising four boys, she could handle it."

"Experience is good. She's not likely to panic if the boys get a little wild."

The sun sank behind them with a softening glow as they drove. Through a wooded copse, a huge white dogwood peeked through other budding tree branches. The red buds, though past their peak, still flashed glorious limbs along the edge. James thought it one of the prettiest Missouri springs he'd seen since he was a boy.

The weekend crowd caused the restaurant service to be slow; neither James nor Alexis noticed. They talked of various things in their lives—teaching, and Alexis's effort to balance her students. The shop, and James's growing workload.

"Trouble is, summers are overloaded with customers wanting service right away, and winters can practically close me down," he muttered. "Seasonal. Another month and I'll have enough business to keep me occupied sixteen hours in the day. Haven't given much thought to what I'll do with Cliff in the summer."

"There's always camp," Alexis suggested between sips of tea.

He liked watching her hands, feminine and a bit delicate. He liked watching her...period.

"There's a thought," he replied. "I'll start asking around. But I'm hoping if Cliff and Robby continue to get along, maybe I can work something out with Robby's mom, Sara. She's a stay-at-home."

"That's a workable solution, too," Alexis offered. "Especially if, as you say, this mom knows how to exert firm boundaries. That way he won't lose ground over the summer."

Her approval sent a warm glow his way.

They barely made the late movie, slipping into back-row seats to view an adventure tale that featured impossible feats by the hero. Alexis giggled over the last-minute rescue ending, and James joined her, finding her uninhibited laughter infectious. He grabbed her hand to pull her from her seat, and kept it in his as they made their way out. They exited the theater still chuckling—

And ran smack into someone Alexis knew. James heard a sharp intake of breath as the woman addressed them.

"Hi, Alexis," the tall, forty-something woman said, and paused, throwing an inquisitive glance at James. Her mouth made a funny little pucker before she asked, "Did you enjoy the movie?"

"Hi, Elizabeth..." Alexis pulled her hand from his and folded her fingers securely around her purse. "Yes, we did, thank you. And you?"

James leaned his weight on one leg and shoved his hands into his pockets. It struck him that Alexis wasn't too happy to see the woman.

"Mmm…it was okay." Elizabeth didn't offer to introduce her male companion. Alexis didn't offer to introduce J.D. "But I've seen better. Well, good night. See you on Monday."

Her dismissive statement hung in the air as the couple headed toward the opposite side of the parking lot.

Alexis said nothing as they walked toward their vehicle. He glimpsed her biting her lip. What was it about seeing the woman that had upset her?

"Guess I don't know everyone in Sunny Creek," James commented as they reached the car. "A teacher?"

"No. She's the school secretary."

He didn't respond. He hadn't recognized her, but most likely Cliff's records had come across her desk. For certain, she knew who he was, and the woman hadn't missed seeing their clasped fingers.

It suddenly hit him. Elizabeth, the school secretary, had not only been surprised at seeing them together, she hadn't approved.

What did that matter? He'd run into a lot of people in the course of his life who hadn't thought much of him. In his younger years, he'd thumbed his nose at them. Having people disapprove of him only bothered him when his mother was alive.

That was long ago and he was older now. His life was his own. Still, the thought crept in—did it bother

Alexis to be seen out socially with him? She was an uptown girl, while he...

Well, she'd come, hadn't she? He'd be hanged if he'd let that wayward thought ruffle him. If Alexis didn't want to date him, all she had to do was say no. He had every intention of keeping it innocent. For now. For as long as he could hold out without wanting more than a kiss.

For the dozenth time in the past month he wondered where that would take them. Putting aside all that she'd done—was doing—for his son's sake, Alexis was a woman easy to care about. He let his glance slip over her as she sat at his side. She'd turned his head quick enough. Yet she remained head and shoulders above him socially.

He shook off his distraction and stuck a CD into the player without looking at it. "Don't know what's here, since this isn't my car."

"Um...if it's hard metal," she said, "I'll take the simple quiet of nothing, if you don't mind."

"What do you like?" Determined to regain their lighthearted mood, he teased, "Are you one of those women who likes nothing but classical stuff?"

"Sometimes. Are you one of those men who likes nothing but country music?"

"No, no. Not...always." Only most of the time, but he didn't see the need to be that honest. Most of the time these past few years he'd had no one to please but himself, and he was beginning to discover how boring that was. "But you can't beat those old Nashville boys. And some of the up-and-coming singers are worth listening to. Don't sell 'em short.''

"I wouldn't dream of it," she bounced back at him. "If you won't shortchange the classics. It can be wonderfully soothing after a frazzled day. Hey, that's a good thing to introduce to Cliff. Many people learn better while listening to classical music.''

"Now, don't go bringing my son into this," he said, grinning. "We're deciding what music we'll be listening to when we're together.''

"Um, what makes you think there's going to be that much time?'' After glancing at him sharply, she returned to shuffling through the dozen CDs. "Your busy season is beginning, remember? Sixteen hours a day? And I usually travel in summer, or study, or…''

He saw her chin harden while a fleeting sadness settled around her mouth. "Anyway, I have yet to sign a contract with Sunny Creek School Board for the next year.''

"You're not worried about it, are you? With teachers in such short supply?''

"Not really. But there's always a chance I'll be offered a teaching position in another district.''

"Let's not think that far ahead. We still have a few weeks till school is out. Let's just have a little fun.'' In his opinion, that was enough. She'd grow tired of helping him with Cliff and bow out of his life.

And maybe she'd just grow tired of *him*. He'd already decided he had nothing to offer her, hadn't he? But he'd have a good time while it lasted—in that innocent way he was sure she'd allow.

He glanced at the clock on the dash. Thirty minutes till he'd say good-night. Thirty minutes until he could kiss her. He wanted to both rush it and prolong the evening. Already, he thought it too short.

He reduced his speed.

"Here's a popular artist," she said, punching the buttons to release the one playing, then placing the new selection in the slot. "Let's see what this one sounds like."

Twenty-five minutes…

Not the words, and not the voice, but the background music is what he heard later in his mind, as he drew her into his arms at her door and kissed her. She leaned eagerly into him as though she'd longed for this moment as much as he.

There weren't any kids to get home to this time. No one to interrupt them, to cut it short. He pressed his mouth gently on hers and rested there, letting the warmth and feeling and scent of her flow down to his toes and back up again. Her lips tasted like sweet cider. They moved on his, communicating something very elemental…a yearning to love…to merge and melt into one.

His temperature rose, giving him cause to think he might explode with shooting fireworks. He slowly let her go. She stepped back, her eyes huge under the dim overhead light on her tiny porch. His heart beat like a tom-tom. They both sucked in air as though starving for oxygen.

He didn't want her to go inside without him. He swallowed hard against voicing the request. It was too soon to expect more with a woman like Alexis. Reaching out, he stroked her cheek. So soft—like the down of a baby duck.

Maybe it would never be the right thing to ask anyway—with a woman like her. This was a woman who kept to her principles. God's principles.

If he'd kept to them ten years ago, Cliff would never have been born. J.D. regretted that now. Not Cliff, but the way he'd been conceived.

"G'night, Alexis…"

"'Night, James."

He forced himself to take another step backward. Then he pivoted, and teetered on the top stair.

The thought of falling all the way down them was enough to yank him out of his dreamy state. A sharp chuckle rose from his middle. Imagine—a kiss that affected him so much it sent him loopy at his age. He wasn't a randy teenager anymore. At this rate he was likely to break his neck.

Random thoughts of all the places he might take her bombarded him like pelting rain. Places that would please her, where nothing from their daily lives would intrude on them. Like that fancy restaurant on the far side of the lake. Or his favorite barbecue restaurant. A boatride at dusk.

"G'night, Alexis…" he muttered again, knowing he'd go home only to dream of the soft curve of her cheek against his palm and the way her lips felt against his.

Then he concentrated on descending the stairs so he wouldn't trip and make a complete fool of himself.

Chapter Ten

Alexis awoke to an insistent ringing. Fumbling for the phone, she brought it to her ear without opening her eyes. "'Lo…"

"Alexis?"

"Hmmm?" She heard a distant tapping. Darkness lay across her bedroom, but outside a single bird chirped. Almost dawn? Who would be calling at dawn?

"It's me, Teach. J.D. Er, James."

The tapping sounded again, and she shot out of bed.

"Somebody's at my door," she muttered into the phone.

"It's only me."

"Is it an emergency?" Grabbing her turquoise print summer robe, she tucked her receiver under her chin as she struggled to get her arms through the sleeves, all the while hurrying to the front of her apartment.

"Nope. Sorry." She heard him take a breath, and

there was a note of regret in his apology. "Didn't aim to scare you."

"What is it, then?" Her pounding heart began to subside a little. She blew a strand of hair out of her eyes.

"Just get dressed. In jeans, your oldest sneakers and warm top layers."

"Why?" She unlocked the door as quickly as possible, blinking away sleep. Cool predawn air hit her face as she swung it wide. She snapped on the light over the door.

"So you can peel off by layers as the day warms." James sported an early-morning beard, and his eyes were shadowed by an old baseball cap.

"That's not what I meant...." She scanned James's face, trying to guess what he was honestly thinking, but his expression didn't reveal anything. Still she probed. "Is something wrong? Is Cliff all right?"

"Yes, he's fine." James disconnected his phone and stuck the tiny implement into his pocket. "Nothing's wrong. We're going fishing."

"Fishing?" Alexis let her mouth drop, disconnected her own phone and tightened her belt. Oh! She had a list of things to take care of, but she was entitled to another two hours of sleep on a Saturday morning. As long as there was no emergency, she planned on going back to bed. "Are you serious?"

"As a state judge."

A huge yawn demanded expression. "But it's not even daylight," she mumbled through it. Their Friday-night date had been a week ago, but they'd talked for a while after the Thursday-night Bible Study. He hadn't said a word about fishing then.

"That's the point. We have to leave now to be on the lake early. I'll give you five minutes to get dressed."

"What makes you think I want to go fishing?" Although she had no objections to others enjoying the sport, she simply didn't feel drawn to participate.

"You aren't going to turn down a chance to learn something new, are you? What will your students say? Most of these kids grow up with lake fishing. You want to relate, don't you?"

"But—" He *was* serious.

"Want to go in your pj's?" His challenging gaze roved down her figure with growing interest, seeming to gauge the thinness of the pajamas beneath her robe. "I might find that interesting, though I don't think it would excite the fish much. Takes more than a pretty woman to fool 'em into taking the bait."

"Don't be silly." She turned away from the door. "I need coffee."

"Four and a half minutes," he said. Although laced with humor, his tone was adamant. "You don't need makeup. Hair brushing is optional. I'll wait for you in the truck, but if you're not down by then, I'm coming back to get you, jeans or not."

She stopped and turned back to the door, protesting, "It takes that long to make coffee."

"We're down to four minutes." He didn't give her an inch to maneuver, even while his grin spread wider. "I think you'll be more comfortable dressed for the lake than in those pajamas. Bring a hat, too, if you have one. And we have coffee in the truck.''

One more protest hovered on her lips, but it didn't take her long to realize James wasn't giving up. So…she might as well be gracious, and go along.

''Five minutes,'' she bargained. She closed her door and dashed to her bedroom.

She actually took seven minutes, but James didn't point that out as she climbed into the truck. Around them in the half light of dawn, the morning bird chorus began.

Her eyes narrowed. ''Are you sure you want me along?''

''I came to get you, didn't I?''

A typical male response, Alexis mused, halfway between amusement and annoyance. Yet she knew it was an honest answer for him. She buckled the seat belt. Noticing a small blue pillow had been added to the front seat, she tucked it between her and the door. ''Where's Cliff?''

''At another sleepover at Robby's house.'' He handed her a large thermos, then, putting the truck in gear, he backed out of the drive. ''There's food in the bag.''

She investigated the brown bag that lay on the seat between them. A warm aroma made her nose twitch. She pulled out foam cups and peeked at what lay beneath. It looked like sandwiches packed from home. ''Is this breakfast or lunch?''

''Both, I'm afraid. I have to be back in town by noon.''

She unscrewed the thermos lid. "How come you have a Saturday morning free?"

"Got a lucky break—"

He came to a silent crossroads and she took the opportunity to pour coffee without spilling it. She handed him a cup as he turned south.

"My old buddy Denny—Dennis Bender—you know, Caroline and Fitz's son? He's in town. He's opening up Sullivan's Repair for me this morning."

"That's nice of him."

"Owed me a favor."

"Oh." She dug into the bag again, pulling out paper towels and the food. "So, where are we going?"

"Not all that far."

"One of your secret places?"

He glanced at her, taking the egg-and-cheese sandwich she handed him. "Did I say I had secret places?"

She settled against the corner and braced her feet against the bounce, munching on her own sandwich. "You mentioned little-known spots where you could be quiet and alone."

He remained thoughtful for a moment, sipping his coffee. "Yeah, I suppose you could call it that. This place can't be reached by a paved road. Some of the land ends in a cliff at the lake and isn't developed. I don't own any of it, but anyone can fish there. Just no one does much."

"So where do you fish from, then?"

"We'll go in by boat."

She remained quiet for a few moments and finished

her breakfast. James drove down a tree-lined private road unknown to her. She hadn't investigated too many of the summer cabins in her season in the area, and there were many around the lake. The lake soon came into view, the v sta widening as they approached a clearing. She rolled down her window to see it better.

Alexis caught her breath at the morning's beauty. She sat straighter to take it in. Streaks of sunlight touched treetops with gold and sparkled like diamonds on the water. A slight breeze stirred, blowing strands of hair across her eyes.

James brought the truck to a halt beside a modest boat landing. Against a hill, in the background of thick trees, sat a very modern cabin. A large log house that looked more like a lodge, with sturdy beams and porch posts, it invited attention. It could be featured in a house and architect magazine, she thought.

"I keep my boat here," he explained, nodding to the low structure beside the floating dock. "And keep track of the place over the winter for the owners."

"Oh. Whose place is this?"

"Galen's. They're not here this weekend."

So this was the Stallings place of which she'd heard. "I didn't realize you have a boat."

He got out, coming around to open her door. "Only a small outboard motor," he said as he unloaded the fishing gear and a cooler from the truck bed. "Don't use it for water-skiing or anything like that. Just fish with it."

"You don't like water sports?"

''They're all right. I've done my share. I don't have time for it, though.''

James led her down the pebble-in-concrete path, then down steps to the covered boat dock. From one of four bays, he loaded the fishing gear and small cooler into a boat.

He helped her into a life jacket, his fingers tickling her chin as he snapped the tabs. Alexis glanced up, thinking he'd done so to tease her, only to entangle her gaze in his. The breeze stirred her hair. He didn't smile as he gently brushed it from her eyes. Letting his dark eyes speak, his thoughts searched hers with wonder. The wonder in her rose and sparked. Her breath caught.

''That should do it,'' he murmured, dropping his hands and breaking the contact. His voice sounded as though he had a burr in his throat. ''Climb in.''

She moistened her lips and started to breathe again.

She followed his instructions and he pushed off. With an economy of movement, James started the motor, backed them out of the dock and turned them out toward the main channel. The wide-open water dwarfed the sound of their puttering motor. Drifting fog hung over the passing inlets.

Alexis wrapped her arms around her knees, shivered a bit against the cool spray and studied James as he lifted his face to catch the early-morning sun. He sniffed the air. He carefully observed the shoreline as they passed. He seemed to look at everything, missing little. Passing a distant fisherman, he waved.

After a few moments, he slowed and guided the

boat into a deep cove, one with a shallow valley between high bluffs. At the valley's edge, old trees and new hung out over the water, and he brought the boat closer to them. He let the anchor sink. Moving with quiet ease, he got out the fishing poles.

James inspected the two, then said, "You can use this one."

"That's okay." She cleared her throat. "I think I'll simply sit here and enjoy the morning while you fish."

"You don't want to try your hand?"

Her tummy dropped nervously. He honestly expected her to fish? She'd never laid claim to being any kind of sportsman. Her dad and uncle had liked occasional fishing, but it had never interested her. She'd been too much of a girly girl, she supposed. Neither of her sisters had been of the tomboy bent either.

"I, um, already told you I don't really like wiggly things."

"Come on, Teach. Think of it as an experience."

"What are you using for bait?" she asked suspiciously.

"The finest worms in the state."

"Real worms?"

"Sure 'nuff." He let a moment go by, then flashed her a teasing glance. "But I'll bait your hook for you."

"Thanks, there, ol' buddy." Her tone wry, she gave him half a pout.

Grinning, James followed through with his promise. Then he showed her how to hold the rod, how the reel worked and how to cast the line. He watched her a moment, then took up his own rod. He settled himself in the forward seat close to the bow.

Alexis remained quiet, ignoring her pole, feeling the soft sway of the boat after a distant wave came their way, letting her gaze feast on his profile. His face in repose grew solemnly content, his eyes focusing often on the middle distance. She wondered what his thoughts were. Wondered why he had brought her on his morning jaunt. But she didn't ask.

"Got one." Startled out of her reverie, she watched as he played the line, then landed a fish. She had no idea what kind it was. She averted her gaze when he removed it from the hook. He put it in his cooler, then painstakingly threaded his hook again. He glanced at her and grinned again. "You do, too."

"What?" She twisted and leaned halfway out of the boat, nearly dropping her rod. "Oh, that thinga-mabob is jumping."

"Uh-huh, it sure is. Reel it in."

She shifted to her knees, holding the rod so tight that her knuckles shown white. The boat rocked.

"Hey, watch out there, Alexis. Sit down."

"But it's going to get away."

James rose to come beside her. "Maybe, but don't lean too far out, will you?"

Alexis tried to follow his coaching, feeling awkward. He placed a palm at her back, but let her handle the rod until she finally got the hang of reeling smoothly. She had been so sure the fish would wriggle off the hook—had been hoping it would—that it surprised her when it did not.

The fish flapped as it came out of the water. Viewing it gave her pause. "Oh, the poor thing…" she murmured. "Maybe I—"

"Don't you dare."

"Um…I…I…"

"Here, give it to me." He took her rod and removed the fish from the hook while Alexis turned away. "We'll have fish for supper."

"I don't know how to do fresh fish properly," she admitted, biting her lip.

"Never mind. I do."

They grew quiet again. James took his place in the bow, ignoring her as he concentrated on fishing. Alexis sat and dreamed, content to contemplate nature's morning activity.

"James, it's bobbing again."

"So, reel it in."

She tried. The line snagged. Scooting closer to the boat's side, she tugged unsuccessfully. She rose to her knees for more leverage, and the boat dipped dangerously. She tried to steady herself, and shifted, but that only sent the boat rocking again.

"Alexis…"

She heard the cautioning tone, but it was too late. With a shriek, she tumbled into the water.

Beneath the surface, she automatically straightened her body, kicked and shot to the surface, coming up giggling. If this wasn't the silliest thing she'd ever done…

If they knew, her students would never let her hear the end of it. Did she have even a shred of hope of James not telling this tale?

"I've got you." His eyes anxious, James reached for her, wrapping his hands around her shoulders. They felt strong and capable. Safe. "Thank heaven you're wearing that life vest."

Sputtering and laughing, she wrapped her hands around the boat rim. "But I am a competent swimmer, even though I'm a poor fisherman."

"Well, I'm glad to hear it," he said with a mixture of humor and vexation, "but I don't advise swimming and fishing in the same outing. Now, let's get you back in the boat."

He set his feet and gave a mighty heave, helping her into the boat. She landed against him, soaking his vest and everywhere she touched. Holding her close, his gaze warmed to brown sugar, and his smile held a world of tantalizing promise.

"Guess it's time to head home." He leaned closer, rubbing his nose lightly against hers, Eskimo style. "I don't think we'll catch any more fish today."

"Just as well," she answered, starting to shiver. "It's too early in the year and too early in the morning for the water to be warm. Besides, I think I'm a lousy fisherman."

"Now, what would you say to one of your kids if they showed that kind of negativity?"

Alexis mumbled something under her breath.

"I didn't hear that," James taunted.

"You rat."

"Now, now. No names." His grin was a running accompaniment with his actions. Pulling off his sweatshirt, he bunched it so that it easily slipped over her head. "That will help some."

He started the motor and took them back to his home dock.

Her clothes stuck to her in various places as she hopped from one foot to the other on their way to the truck. She climbed into the vehicle in total disgust. She'd ruined his morning.

"Sorry about your quiet morning, James."

"What do you mean?"

"You only caught two fish."

"There will be other mornings." He tossed her another grin as he pointed the truck back toward town. "And lots more fish in the lake. But I don't think there will ever be a funnier sight than you going over the side of the boat."

Alexis couldn't prevent a groan. "I suppose you'll spend the next decade telling the yarn about dunking the teacher too dumb to fish."

"I don't know about that," he said, his voice soft. "The surprise on your face was beyond the telling. I think I'll simply savor it for a while. Some things don't need to be shared."

He was still amused, she noted. But his glance held tenderness as well. Somewhere in that disguise of a sometimes brusque, no-nonsense approach to life lived a man capable of a great deal of love. Did James know that about himself?

Perhaps they wouldn't reel in more fish this morning, but Alexis wasn't all that sure he hadn't made a cast for her heart.

She definitely felt the tug of a hook.

Chapter Eleven

A week later, Alexis perched on a kitchen stool, sipping her coffee, while she thought about the upcoming weekend. She'd planned to run up to her parents' house, but now she didn't want to go. With only weeks of school left, there were several things to wrap up here. Plus there were…other things keeping her here. For one, James had missed the Thursday-night Bible Study, and she'd promised to type her notes to help him catch up.

She imagined spending extra time helping James study Hebrews. Just the two of them…

Nibbling a slice of toast, she pushed the thought around. Why was he so…interesting? James wasn't at all her type of man—she usually went for men who were career oriented. And she and James had had only two genuine dates!

And a few kisses—three, to be exact. Kisses that sent her reeling.

With a twist of her mouth, she wadded her paper napkin and gathered up her dishes. She didn't want to examine that thought too closely. The kisses from James made her nervous, even as she wanted more. But after the school year ended, there might never be another kiss. Even with her former plans to get married up in smoke, she wasn't likely to hang around Sunny Creek for the summer. What would she do here without school in session? What would keep her?

By the time she returned next year, nothing much would be left of this attraction between her and James. Next year would change everything. Every school year had its own personality, its own makeup of students and parents. Cliff would have a different teacher.

Under the circumstances, that was better.

Anyway, a purely physical attraction wasn't enough to build a lifetime on. There had to be more.

Sighing, she washed her few dishes. She did have to finish those vests by the end of the week.

She'd better let her mother know not to expect her. Alexis punched in her parents' phone number, ready with a long explanation. "Hi, Mom. I—"

"Oh, Alexis, honey," her mother interrupted. "I was just about to call you. I know you were planning to come home this weekend, but Dad and I have to fly out to Denver. Your aunt Helen has taken a fall, and I fear she's broken a hip."

"Oh dear." Alexis sank down on the edge of her bed. "That's too bad. Is she going to be all right?"

"The doctor says it may take some time for her to recover," her mom rushed on to say. "And she has good care, I'm sure, but I think we need to be there to make sure she's all right. We're family.''

"Yes, I can see that you need to go."

"The only thing is, your sister can't take care of Pepper…''

Pepper, a small black schnauzer, had been the family dog since Alexis was thirteen. Old now, he was babied by her mom, who claimed Pepper was a good stand-in until she had grandchildren.

"That is a problem. How about I come and get Pepper and bring him back with me?" It was an easy decision to make. Her landlady had never told her she couldn't have pets. Pepper would be fine.

"Oh, but what will you do with him while you're at school?"

"I'll manage, Mom," she said, even as that very thought troubled her. What *would* she do with Pepper while she was at school? "Just don't worry. I'll take care of Pepper."

Her mother sighed with relief. "That's a big help, Alexis. What time will you get here?"

"Right about lunchtime, I guess."

"Oh, that will work out just fine, then. And by the way, Ron called."

Alexis remained silent for a moment. She hadn't spoken with Ron since they'd called everything off. "What did he want?"

"Wanted to know when you'd be home next. Said he liked Dallas and his new job. Said he missed you. He left a number." When Alexis didn't immediately answer, her mom asked, "Do you want it?"

There had been no commitment left between them by the time Ron moved to Dallas. In fact, they had agreed to date other people, and she had rather thought he had someone in mind in his new location. In any case, he hadn't been too keen on reaching her and hadn't been in touch since before spring break.

And not very often even then. Before their breakup, she'd done most of the calling.

A balloon of irritation and sadness rose up to mock her. Why had she ever thought he'd make a good husband for her? Had she been totally fooling herself, seeing qualities that weren't there? She could see it clearly now.

He'd never been too keen about marriage. He'd been so lukewarm, that now she thought he'd dribble through anything.

"Dear?" her mother prompted.

"No," Alexis said finally. She felt no urgent desire to talk with Ron. "I'll get his number while I'm there."

She concluded her conversation and put it out of her mind. If she was going to make the two and a half hour trip home after all, she had to speed up the morning.

She began to pack her overnight bag, then stopped. She always felt comfortable at the church she'd grown up in, and loved her friends there, but she suddenly didn't want to miss Sunday services in Sunny Creek. She'd become attached to the people, the members with whom she shared Bible Study and prayers and worship.

And she didn't want to miss seeing James. That was the kicker. He'd been attending steadily for several weeks now. A spiritual fledgling, learning to walk. It wasn't hard for her to admit she enjoyed his growing presence in her life. It was only hard to decide where it was going. Or if she needed to retreat.

That disturbed her more than she liked.

Dressing in jeans and T-shirt, and grabbing an over-size shirt just in case, she headed out the door to her car.

She was a block from her house when her cell phone rang. "Yes?"

"It's J.D. Uh, James." She could hear buzzing noises in the background. Then a faint slam.

"Hi, James. I'm about three minutes away. I have those study notes you wanted. I'm dropping them off before I leave town for the day."

"You are? Tried you at home just a minute ago. Wait a minute—" The phone was smothered, yet she heard him caution Cliff to quiet down. He came back on, his voice lowered to a husky tone. "Wanted to say I had a good time the other night—just talking."

"Me, too. I…" The background noise increased as she drove. "So, Cliff is with you?"

"Um, yeah. Cliff spent last night at Robby's house, but he's here with me now. Hold on—" There was a *crash*, followed by the sound of a banging door.

"Cliff!"

"Daaad?" came a faint wail.

"Oh, no… Gotta go."

"Never mind, James. I'll be right there." She cut the connection, but he'd already gone.

Two blocks later, she parked in front of James's shop. She scrambled out of her seat and swung through the shop door.

Cliff stood toward the back of the shop, shifting from one foot to the other. He was crying, strands of his long hair in his eyes. "Honest, I didn't do nothing to it. I flushed it twice, but it just wouldn't flush right."

From the back room, James's agitated voice drifted out to her. "I've told you a dozen times, Cliff, not to fiddle with it!"

She laid a hand on Cliff's shoulder. "What's the matter? What happened?"

Cliff's face turned her way, tears tracking down his cheeks. "It just broke, Miss Richmond. Honest. It wasn't my fault."

"It broke because you couldn't keep your hands out of the holding tank," James yelled at him. "If this isn't a—"

His angry words suddenly became unintelligible, and Alexis thought it just as well. She peeked around the corner to the back room. The door to the bathroom was open; James was bent over the commode, the back of which was off. Wet splotches dotted his jeans. Water crept over the cement floor, pooling into the workroom in wider circles by the second.

"But I was trying to make it work," Cliff insisted. His dark brown eyes looked tired. They begged for understanding.

"Stubborn kid. I told you the plumbing was old and not to mess with it, didn't I?" James glanced at them over his shoulder. His mouth twisted with disgust. "I shut off the valve, but something's sprouted a leak. Would you just look at this mess?"

"Why don't we get out of the doorway," Alexis said hastily, pulling Cliff back into the shop's reception area.

Just then, the phone rang at the same time that the bell dinged on the shop's outside door. An older man came in, hefty in build and tanned. He glanced about and then at Alexis and Cliff, his curiosity heightening as his gaze connected with hers.

Then he called, "J.D., you here?"

"That you, Wiley?" James shouted back. "Be there in a sec."

The phone rang for a third time.

"Uh, should I come back?" Wiley asked, his expression puzzled yet still curious.

On the fourth ring, Alexis stepped over to the phone and snatched up the receiver. "Sullivan's Repair."

James came around the corner into view, wiping his hands on a clean rag. He paused, his eyes harried as he glanced around him. Another moment or two and the water would seep past the back room.

"Might be better if you can wait," he told Wiley. "Gotta get a plumber in here."

"Sure, J.D. Get Mac if you got a plumbing problem," Wiley said, making no move to leave. "These old buildings are always in need of some repair. Mac knows about this old stuff."

Cliff began to edge away, eyeing the three feet of space between his dad's back and the door to the back room. Beyond was the door to the back alley.

Alexis listened to what the phone customer wanted and searched for a pen as she kept her gaze on Cliff's movements. She suspected the boy wanted a quick getaway. He'd tried that tactic a couple of times the first week of school.

"Will do," James agreed. Without turning, he reached out and laid a hand on the boy's shoulder, effectively halting Cliff's hope for freedom.

Alexis made a quick note, then hung up. She didn't know who Mac was, but thought the town's ol' boy network had sprung into place.

"I'm headed down that way. Want I should tell Mac you need him quick? Looks like you've got your hands full." Wiley finished his offer with another glance at Alexis.

"Yeah, Wiley. You do that. That would be good."

Wiley ambled out of the store, and James turned to Alexis. "Thanks for getting the phone."

"No problem with that," she said, handing him the message. "What can I help you with?"

"Nothing you can do. I'll have to close the shop. This plumbing problem will take up the whole day, I'm thinking."

"I can help you mop up."

"Nah. I have a Wet Vac that can do the job. If Mac can get over here sometime before the morning's over, maybe it won't be so long."

James turned his son to face him. His mouth tightened.

The boy looked miserable. "Honest, Dad…"

Some of James's ire faded. "Cliff—"

"Why don't I take Cliff with me?" she quickly suggested. "I have to run up home to my parents' house and pick up my dog. My parents are going out of town and they don't like to put him in a kennel if they can avoid it. Poor old Pepper doesn't do well there."

"Alexis, I can't ask you to do that. You wrestle kids all week."

"You didn't ask. I offered." She gazed at Cliff a moment. The child was stressed. James was frazzled. Yet his wrath had carried no promise of a physical threat, she noted. She thought it remarkable that he'd made real strides in so short a time. "Besides, I think I'd like company on the drive, and Cliff can help me with Pepper."

"Are you sure?" James gazed at her as though she might have lost her mind.

"Yes, I'm sure. But we'll be gone all day."

"It will make a long Saturday for you."

"You already have a long Saturday in progress." Alexis glanced behind him at the water now seeping through the doorway into the main shop room. It was a mess, all right.

And Cliff… Ever mindful of the moods of her students, she'd noticed Cliff's fretfulness ever since she arrived. She turned to the boy. "Cliff, hon, have you taken your meds today?"

Cliff hopped from one foot to the other. His gaze flashed from her to his dad, revealing his worried state. "Uh...uh...I don't remember."

"That's it." James hit the heel of his hand against his forehead. "I should've realized it. Cliff, didn't Robby's mom...?" Guilt flashed across his face. "Never mind. The fault is mine. I forgot to make sure she knew about it. Where is it, son?"

Alexis gave James an approving smile for his softened tone. He did seem to be learning forbearance.

"Um...in my backpack, I guess."

"Well, dig it out. You'll be ten in a few weeks. Old enough to remember it without prompting," Alexis said with a teasing smile, turning responsibility back into Cliff's keeping. She ruffled his hair. "As soon as you take it, we'll scoot out of here."

A hopeful expression traveled over the boy's features as he turned his gaze toward his dad for his blessing.

"Sure, okay, son. Get your meds and you can go."

Cliff slept a good part of the trip to Kansas City. That was fine with Alexis. He'd be on his better behavior if rested. She woke him just before they reached her parents' home.

"Almost there, Cliff."

When they arrived, he looked about with a keen curiosity as they entered the large ranch-style house. Alexis didn't place a lot of restraints on his natural curiosity. She introduced him to her mother, then to Pepper. Pepper jumped and sniffed, making friends quickly. Cliff dropped to the floor and started petting him.

"Where's Dad?" Alexis asked.

"Out on last-minute errands," Connie Richmond responded. She was a smaller version of her three daughters, blond and perky, and loved playing the family matriarch like a queen.

She was very proud of her daughters, and touted Eileen's recent promotion as director of nursing at the huge retirement home where she worked, and Janet's business acumen. But she often voiced her complaint over not yet having grandchildren.

Alexis and her sisters always pretended to groan when anyone told them how much they were like their mother, but, truthfully, none of them really minded.

"I've packed up some dog food for you, and Pepper's vitamins," Connie continued while making sandwiches. "His traveling cage is clean and ready to go. You can take his bedding, too. It'll help him settle in a strange place."

"When are you flying out, Mom?" Alexis asked, automatically setting three places at the breakfast counter in the large sun-yellow kitchen. "You didn't have to bother with lunch for us when you're in a hurry."

"No trouble, really. We're packed. We do have to leave for the airport in a couple of hours, though. Now that you're here," her mother said, and changed direction from one breath to the next, "are you planning to stay around for a bit? Would you mind doing *something* with that box of stuff you left after spring break?

I'm in the middle of redecorating the house, and your old room is my next project. You know the one.''

The box into which she'd thrown keepsakes of her time with Ron. After they'd broken up, she'd impulsively gathered everything in sight to do with wedding plans and tossed them into a cardboard box. She'd left it sitting in a corner of her old room.

Alexis glanced at Cliff. He seemed content for the moment. ''Sure, Mom. I might as well take that with me, too. I'll be able to sort it out later.''

It suddenly dawned on Alexis that the prospect no longer troubled her as it had a mere couple of months back. It would be simply another chore to do.

As they ate their lunch, Pepper settled near Cliff's tall kitchen stool. Pepper was a master at begging.

Cliff looked at her. ''Can I feed him?''

''Sure, but why don't you give him some dog bones?'' Alexis said, an idea forming. ''He'll love you forever.''

As the two women cleared the lunch dishes, Cliff and Pepper played in the backyard.

''Mom, if it's all right with you, I'll pick up Pepper later. I'm going to take Cliff to the zoo for a couple of hours. I think we'll both enjoy it.''

''That's fine, hon. Pepper can remain home alone for a few hours. But if you're very late, Dad and I will be gone.''

''I have my key,'' Alexis reminded her.

''That will be fine,'' Connie said, hanging a dish towel on the drying rack. ''And before I forget…

here's Ron's number. He said to tell you to call him.''

Alexis tucked the number into her purse without looking at it. She had more important things on her mind. She hadn't been to the zoo in ages, and it had been one of her favorite places to go as a kid. Eagerly, she called Cliff in to wash his hands and face.

Chapter Twelve

They started home from the zoo late in the afternoon. Alexis felt pleased with their spontaneous excursion. They'd spent longer at the zoo than she'd originally intended, but when Cliff became fascinated with the exhibits, she couldn't bear to tear him away before he'd had his fill. He'd been so cute, she could hardly wait to share it with James.

After viewing the various monkeys and apes, Cliff declared those his favorite animals. Then the elephants were the best animal ever.

When they watched the seals being fed, he stated he could swim that well and he'd seen wild ones one time in California. They were his favorites.

But then again, giraffes were really cool. He wanted to grow a neck that tall so he could see over everything.

Last but not least, he wanted to roar like a lion and be the king, like in the animated movie.

Alexis chuckled at his declarations all the way back to pick up Pepper, teasing and joking with him as she normally couldn't do in the classroom. He laughed and teased back, his eyes bright with joy.

At Cliff's begging, she allowed the boy and Pepper to share the back seat, but instructed Cliff to keep Pepper calm.

Perhaps this outing was one of God's blessings in disguise, Alexis mused as she set Pepper's traveling cage in her front seat, and his bedding, food dishes and food in the trunk. The huge cardboard box that represented her recent hopes and dreams she shoved into the corner.

Finally packed for the trip back, she called James. "Hi. We're just starting home."

"Glad to know where you are. You forgot to leave your parents' number, and I don't have your cell phone number either."

"Oh, I'm sorry, James. That was irresponsible of me. Well, take down my cell number." She gave it, then asked, "How's it going at the shop?"

"Good as can be expected. Sam got the leak fixed for now, anyway."

"For now, huh. More work to be done?"

"Is that my dad?" Cliff leaned forward to ask.

She nodded, and started the car as she listened to James. She edged to the end of the drive.

"There is quite a lot of work, actually," James said. "This whole line of buildings need improvements, and so far none of the other tenants nor I have been able to get Old Man Baker, the owner, to do much."

"So, what's to be done?"

"Can I talk to my dad?" Cliff implored.

"We've called a meeting with the old miser. Guess we'll have to see what comes of that. Say, Alexis... why don't I meet you and Cliff someplace for dinner?"

"Actually, that's a great idea. Tell you what, Cliff wants to talk— You two can decide where to eat while I drive. See you soon."

She handed the phone over her shoulder, then pulled out on the street. Cliff chatted enthusiastically about the zoo for a couple of blocks, then, spotting a couple of teens on skateboards, he twisted around to watch them. "Dad, can I have a new skateboard?"

Alexis didn't know what James answered, but she heard the disappointment as Cliff answered in monosyllables. "Okay...bye."

"Dad says to meet him at that restaurant on the corner out on the highway. He said can you be there at eight."

Two hours later, she wedged her car into a narrow space at the designated restaurant. A handful of people lounged outside the door. Saturday night brought everyone out, she knew.

James wrenched her door open as she released her seat belt. Then he opened the back door. Cliff bounced out and Pepper barked, excitedly wagging his tail.

"Isn't he cool, Dad? Miss Richmond says he's an old man in doggie years, but he still likes to play."

James gave a slow grin. He glanced her way. "I've

heard that. That some old dogs like to play until their last day.''

''Well, this one is tired of being pinned down and wants a quick run,'' she replied with a lift of her brow, trying hard not to let him see how much his grin affected her. Or that she wished to play, too, if it meant with him. She nodded toward the front door. ''How long is the wait? Do we have time to let Pepper out for a bit?''

''I think so.'' He checked his watch. ''Should be about another ten minutes before they call us.''

They let Cliff attach Pepper's leash, then walked toward the side street, away from the busy highway. Cliff waited patiently while Pepper sniffed and paused, discovering new territory.

''Are you tired?'' James asked, his glance inquisitive.

''A bit. But, James, you should've seen Cliff at the zoo. I could barely pull him away from it. At one point I thought he might climb over into the African exhibit. Had to hang on to his shirt.''

She chuckled at the recollection. Teaching a child such as Cliff was always a challenge. But Cliff said he'd never been to a zoo. Surely he'd been to one sometime. Perhaps he just didn't remember. Still, she couldn't help asking.

''Didn't his mother ever take him to a California zoo?''

''Don't know. She…we…'' James paused, his lips twisting in contempt as he struggled to explain. ''We didn't talk much. My fault. I know that. We married too young, I guess, and I'm not much of a talker.''

He smiled ruefully. ''Usually.''

He grew silent, watching Cliff and Pepper. Alexis wondered if his memories were too painful to recount. Did he still grieve over his ex-wife? Over their separation? Why hadn't his marriage lasted? Perhaps, as he said, he had a hard time expressing his deeper emotions.

Then he continued in a low voice. ''I worked two jobs, see. Barely made ends meet sometimes. I was too tired to talk, and Melanie…''

He let it go and shoved his hands into his pockets. They paced to the corner and started back toward the restaurant.

''But the few times I tried it,'' he started again, ''it seemed we had nothing to say. Then they left. Went out to California. When I could, I called. Melanie always said Cliff was fine, that she got the support check, or she called me if it was late. That was it.''

''Didn't she talk about the things they did?''

''Nope. Never wanted Cliff to stay on the phone long,'' he murmured. Cliff was about ten feet in front of them. ''If she and I talked, too often it ended in a fight.''

''Oh…I'm sorry, I didn't mean to pry in…in that direction.''

''It's ancient history now. Guess we never did talk much. She used to fuss at *that* all the time.'' In the lights from the cafe, his eyes shone with self-discovery. ''Then, after she moved, she wouldn't talk either. Said I had no business interfering in her life. I didn't know much about her job or the other guys she dated. Didn't know she was sick. If she'd told me…if I'd known, I'd have brought Cliff home sooner. Instead I heard about it from a stranger. She was gone before I could help.''

Alexis could only imagine the nightmare that kind of situation made for a parent. Guilt, too.

They coaxed Pepper back toward the car. Alexis opened her trunk to dig out a couple of dog biscuits. "Cliff, find that jug of water we brought, will you? Pepper needs a drink.''

She helped the boy find the water dish and fill it. James leaned against her car and watched Pepper lap his fill.

Someone called out, "Sullivan, party of three.''

"That's us.''

Alexis put Pepper back in her car, cracked the back window for air, then locked it. Then the three of them headed inside.

"I'll follow you home to help you with those boxes and stuff," James said as they climbed into their respective vehicles later that evening.

"That's not really necessary, James.''

"Won't take much time," he insisted.

Alexis shrugged. She started her car and drove to her apartment. James followed and parked his truck in back of her vehicle in the drive. He exited, leaving his door ajar.

"He's asleep," he told her quietly, tipping his head toward Cliff in the truck.

"As quickly as I can shower and settle Pepper, I will be, too," she admitted with a yawn as she popped the trunk. She grabbed the dog's pillow in one hand, then opened the back door to scoop up Pepper, while James took the cage and bag of canned dog food. "I appreciate this. I'm not sure I would push getting it all upstairs tonight on my own."

"It's the least I can do."

They climbed the stairs and she set the pillow on the floor of the tiny porch while she let them in. Pepper wriggled with excitement and began to whimper. Alexis snapped on lights. "I'll put him in the bathroom until I unload the rest of the stuff," she said.

"Never mind. You stay here. I'll get it."

Alexis kept up a soothing croon to help Pepper calm down, and as soon as James reentered the apartment with his dishes, she gave the dog food and water.

James came in a third time carrying the big box from her front seat. "Where do you want this one?"

"Oh…just set it on the floor beside the couch, please."

He complied, but she noticed his curiosity at the contents as part of the lid flipped open. His stare remained fixed for a moment. She couldn't recall what lay on top. Pictures of her and Ron, guest lists, pictures of fabulous houses torn from magazines, samples of invitations—she'd tossed them into the box willynilly.

He glanced at her, questions hovering, brown eyes bright. He didn't ask about the contents. Not a thing.

"Gotta go and get Cliff into bed," he said, his gaze shuttering. "Uh, thanks for taking him for the day. Guess we'll have to try that zoo thing again sometime."

"I was happy to do it, James." She moved toward him, intending to walk him down to his vehicle. "Thanks for hauling all my stuff up."

"Yeah. Sure." He turned abruptly, with a, "See you in the morning," and was out the door in a few long strides.

Cliff came awake barely long enough for James to get him into bed. Between his late night with his friend Robby and the long activity-filled day with Alexis, the boy was worn out.

James shucked his clothes and pulled on a pair of lounging bottoms—something he'd adopted after Cliff came to live with him. He glanced at the old desk. His monthly bills lay there. He needed to get started on them.

Memories flooded him. His dad had always hollered about bills. He'd sit at that desk and snarl if his mom made an extra long-distance phone call to James's Grandma. His mouth and eyes got mean if she spent more than five bucks over her grocery allowance. Made his mom miserable, the old man did, always carping about money.

It was that thrift, though, that had paid for their small house. It didn't surprise James that not one penny was owed when it came to him four years back. He imagined his dad having a hissy fit even in his grave, knowing his mom willed him the house. His dad didn't believe in gaining something unearned, and James hadn't earned even a drop of his respect. In his youth, James had gone from job to job, always working against predictions that he wouldn't amount to anything.

Well, I'm living my life my own way, Pop....

Half the sum James realized from the sale lay in a savings for Cliff.

The other half had funded Sullivan's Repair and his investment in tools. One day he'd save enough money to underwrite the testing of his improvement for the four-stroke engine design that came out a few years ago. That one day lay far off, though, and he had other things on his mind.

He flicked on his TV, surfing lazily through the choices, then clicked it off. Nothing appealed to him. He prepared for bed a scant hour later. He could do with a decent night's sleep himself.

Sleep wouldn't come.

He flopped onto his back. Shoving his hands behind his head, he blinked at the ceiling. Only a night-light from the bathroom, placed there after Cliff came to him, gave illumination.

Troubles with his shop weren't the half of it. Larger living quarters—now that's what they needed. And that would take some cash and contemplation. Not too many apartment buildings in town. There were those apartments similar to Alexis's place—but that one certainly was too small. This rental house wasn't much better, though, for the two of them. Four rooms, if the kitchenette counted. He and Cliff were fine for now, but a growing boy needed more than a bed in a portioned-off section of the living room.

In the dark, he grinned at nothing. *He* was that "growing boy." In his effort to balance his evenings, he'd given Cliff his bedroom.

Then his grin faded. If he'd ever thought there would be a time when he saw Alexis as a guest here, that had faded like a winter sunset on a cloudy day.

There was another guy in her life. Alexis was getting married.

His stomach twisted into a knot. He slung a hand over his eyes.

Why hadn't she told him? She hadn't seemed that kind of woman, to string two men along at the same time. He'd gone and made a brainless fool of himself over her. Imagined she liked him. Imagined that the draw between them was special and went past their differences.

He hated being made to feel stupid, and he felt stupid now. Messing with a woman who belonged to another man was something he didn't do. No, sir. Not his style.

But merely kissing Alexis touched off a fire between them, and he could easily fantasize how it might be if they carried it further. He thought she felt it, too. She'd kissed him with an equal fervency that last time.

But what about those things in that box?

His teeth clamped together. Evidence didn't lie.

But…she wore no ring. She had never mentioned a fiancé, didn't talk about another man and sure didn't act engaged. But what did he know of her life, or who she knew in the big city? Alexis could have a whole string of men standing in line for her in Kansas City, for all he knew. Women lied sometimes.

Why, then, did Alexis seem content here in Sunny Creek? She'd made friends here.

Some of those friends he knew. Caroline. Lori. He'd counted himself as a friend. Alexis had that ability. She made him feel easy, made him think they shared some humor, that they were friends as well as…as…*a man and woman falling in love….*

He wanted to be her lover, that sure was obvious. But he wanted her friendship, her respect, as well. He thought he had been building that with Alexis.

Now he simply didn't know anything, and the feeling left him helplessly vulnerable.

He *hated* feeling helpless. It had driven him to some rash choices when young. He always had to do something to try to exert control over his life, and that often brought on trouble. Some things, his mother had told him when he was sixteen, you had to put into God's keeping and then leave them there.

She'd looked at him as though her heart would break, and that's when J.D. knew he had to straighten out his behavior. For her sake, he'd tried.

Now he was trying again. Going to church. Staying out of trouble with the women.

Lord, I sure do need Your input again. I was an

out-and-out failure as a husband once. I'm not too keen on getting married again. Don't mind admitting it scares me. Scared about being a dad, too. I'm trying my best with Cliff. Don't know from one day to the next if I'm a good father or not, but I'm trying.

Now this woman…You know her…Alexis Richmond. I just have to ask You…what were You thinking when You made our paths cross? Just give me a clue. Please?

He closed his eyes and let out his breath. Only God knew the temptation she brought him. He would have to work hard to resist it.

Chapter Thirteen

The last bit of braid lay smoothly stitched on the very last vest. Alexis stood up and stretched, letting her satisfaction in completing the time-consuming project settle over her.

The other members of the sewing team had various demands on their time tonight, so she had volunteered to stay and finish the last two vests. She sure hoped the school appreciated her efforts. Every bit of her extra time this week had gone to complete the work.

Alexis glanced out of the huge double windows in the teachers lounge. Almost seven, and the May sunlight still streamed through, flooding the room with early-evening sunlight. It was her reason to finish the work at school. She found the natural light much easier to sew by than what her tiny apartment yielded.

When she could afford a home of her own, she'd find one with lots of windows, she vowed. And large rooms.

Around her, quiet reigned, a counterpoint to the usual buzz. Everyone had gone home except for her and the building maintenance man, Mr. Dobbs. As far as she knew, he and a helper were preparing the gymnasium for tomorrow night's program. Pepper lay at her feet, content to remain close. As soon as the students left for the day, she'd run home to feed him and bring him back with her.

She sighed, hanging the vest on the rack with the other thirty-three glossy gold-print ones. Lined up next to them were the triple-shaded satin-blue vests that the sixth graders would wear.

Alexis supposed she'd attend the concert. She liked keeping up with her former students. One of her students from last school year had mainstreamed at the beginning of this one, and that youngster was now in the choir.

She often wished more of her kids could return to a normal school classroom, and frequently prayed for them to make the strides necessary to do that—even knowing most of them never would. Mainly she prayed for them to have their needs met in whatever situation they were in.

Like Cliff. He seemed to be settling down a good bit, but still sometimes had problems getting along on the playground. He also had trouble cooperating in a group game. Cliff knew nothing of diplomacy, either, especially if any of the other students opposed him. He and Tyler never got along. She'd had to give them both another detention yesterday.

Hopefully, some of that belligerence Cliff used

would soften with time as the other kids grew to accept him. Cliff still qualified as the "new kid" in school.

That didn't explain the silence from his dad. Her puzzlement over nearly a week's silence from James surfaced. It hadn't occurred to her there might be a real problem with James until today.

Why hadn't he written her a note this week? Or called her? She'd heard nothing from James since Saturday night. She didn't count Sunday morning worship; he and Cliff had arrived late and left quickly after the close of the service. He'd barely spoken to her.

She'd been a tad hurt over that, but she brushed it aside, knowing how busy he was. But not a single note the following days?

Was he avoiding her?

Alexis pushed her hair out of her eyes and began to pick up all the sewing mess: threads, scissors, pins. The extra bits of fabric went into a bag for Judy, the mother in charge.

A slight rustling from the hall caused Pepper to raise his head. A second later, he rose and trotted to the closed door. He started to bark.

Mr. Dobbs must be in the hall, Alexis thought, and paid little attention. "Shh, quiet, boy. It's only Mr. Dobbs. He won't bother us."

Someone rapped on the door. Pepper continued to bark. "Okay, Pepper boy, I've got it."

She reached the door as it swung open and a pair

of dark eyes peered around the door frame. She jerked her hand away and stepped back.

"Teacher, you planning to spend the night here?"

"James! You startled me." She combed her fingers through her hair, brushing it back from her face, wondering if her heart was beating from fright or from excitement at seeing this man who took up all too many of her thoughts.

"Quiet, boy. It's all right," she commanded. Then to James she said, "What are you doing here?"

He didn't offer an excuse for the recent lapse in their communication, and she couldn't bring herself to mention it herself. Especially since he gazed at her as though his silence meant nothing at all.

Or everything.

Perhaps it made sense only to him, she mused. He did puzzle her. There was a lot she didn't know about James Dean Sullivan.

His slow smile spread, causing her heart to do a somersault. He wore a new pair of jeans and a black checked cotton shirt. He sported a fresh haircut, she noted. His hair lay brushed close against his head.

"Came by to check on you when Cliff said something about you doing homework at school with some other teachers." As he stepped through the door, he glanced at the scattered scraps next to her sewing machine on the lunch table. Who had he been expecting to see? "That sewing again, huh? Is the machine working all right?"

"Yes, very well for an old machine. Is that why you came by?"

"Not exactly. Just cruising. Didn't see any other cars in the lot, so I thought I'd better come in to check if everything was okay. Had to raise Dobbs to let me in."

Pepper sat almost on Alexis's feet, his eyes never leaving James. "I have Pepper with me," she pointed out.

"I see that. Hiya, boy." James dropped to his haunches to pet the dog. "How have you been? Cliff has talked about you all week."

Pepper wagged his tail and licked his hand.

"Oh, he's a fine watchdog," James said wryly.

Alexis chuckled. Pepper loved everyone. "Traitor."

"Where is everybody?" James asked, his brow raised.

"Oh—Judy had an emergency, and the other teacher…" She shrugged. "What does it matter? I had some time on my hands and offered to finish the vests. They're done now, and they'll last the school through several years. The kids will look so spiffy for their concert tomorrow night, I'm sure they'll sing their hearts out."

"Well, are you free now?"

"Free?"

"For the Bible Study. It's Thursday, remember?"

That brought her a smile of a different kind. Only a few weeks ago, she'd been the one urging a reluctant James to attend. "Of course I remember."

He tipped his head and studied her, his eyes softening with concern. "We have thirty minutes. Are you too wiped out to go?"

"No, of course not." She wouldn't miss it for all the chocolate-cashew clusters in town, but especially not these days when James attended. With his frequent questions and comments he kept the study interesting. Stimulating. Even the others had noticed.

His very presence stimulated her....

Shoving that fleeting realization aside, she prevaricated. "But I have to finish picking all this stuff up. I can't leave it in a mess to become a problem in the morning for the other teachers. And I'll have to take Pepper home."

"Tell you what. I'll take Pepper to play with Cliff at my place and come back to get you."

His place. She'd sometimes wondered what his place was like. He'd spoken of his landlady neighbor, whom he hired to sit with Cliff when he needed her, but he'd said little of his living arrangements. Alexis suspected that until Cliff came to live with him, James did most of his living at his shop.

"Well, that's kind of you, James. I'm sure Pepper will like a romp with Cliff. But I'll, uh, meet you at church. Then I can pick Pepper up on my way home."

"Suit yourself. Come on, boy." He scooped Pepper up and pivoted to leave. "But if you're not there by seven-forty, I'll come get you. You shouldn't be hanging around an empty school alone after dark."

He was out the door before Alexis could reply, and she wasn't certain just how to take his sudden dictate. She'd always been perfectly capable of looking after herself, she mused, and it felt strange to have someone so concerned for her safety.

It felt nice. More than nice…

Hastily, she finished cleaning up the remains of the sewing. It wouldn't do to worry anyone.

James waited beside his truck, but not very patiently. He'd give her three minutes more. All the other members of their study group had arrived and gone inside.

Something had nettled him all week long. He was so cotton-picking bothered by what he'd seen in that box of stuff he'd carried into her apartment that he'd broken a prime rule he'd adopted long ago for his dating life. He called someone who might tell him…things. He had to talk to someone who knew Alexis and knew what those pictures meant. Those wedding invitations.

Last night about ten, he'd put his pride on the line. He'd called Lori.

"Honestly, J.D.," Lori told him when he asked her, clear amusement in her voice, "I don't know that much about him. You didn't expect Alexis not to have had boyfriends, did you?"

"Don't be dense, Lori. I'm only asking about this one."

"Oh, well. His name is Ron something, and he has a good position with a marketing firm. That's it. That's all I know."

James hated himself for prying, knew he'd regret pumping Lori for information, knew she'd never let him hear the last of it, yet he couldn't resist asking, "Are you sure they've broken up?"

"I don't know details, J.D., but Alexis said they had. I never met the guy and she never wore a ring. All I know is she came back and said the wedding was off."

"How…how upset was she?"

"Now, that's funny, J.D."

Lori never could resist a good tease. Prepared to suffer it through, James rubbed the back of his neck and listened.

"You of all people worrying about someone taking a romance seriously."

"C'mon, Lori." He lightened his tone. "I didn't say Alexis and I had something going, now, did I?"

Lori burst out laughing. "Um…J.D., I didn't mean *your* romance. I don't even pretend to keep up with yours or Denny's. I meant since when did you pay attention to *any* twosome."

James grimaced. If Lori only knew how stark his life had become these past few years. Yet, he could allow his friend her outdated illusions, he supposed.

"Uh, not often. But do I have to have a reason for wanting to know about my son's teacher?" He settled more comfortably on the plaid couch in his living room. "About a woman who has a great deal of interest in his welfare at the moment?"

"Uh-huh." Lori's voice was positively lilting. "Well, the reputation of the J. D. Sullivan I know isn't usually all that innocent, now is it? So is Cliff the real reason you want to know about Alexis's love life?"

That made him squirm, but he answered honestly. "All right, you win. I have another reason for wanting to know about Alexis. Now tell me—was she much torn up or not over this Ron guy?''

Lori put aside her teasing. ''She wasn't nearly as upset as I would be, J.D. Guess there wasn't a true engagement there, after all. If you're all that interested in Alexis, why don't you ask her?''

''Yeah. Suppose I should,'' he'd said with an implied shrug. ''Sometime. But do me a favor and don't tell anyone I've been asking, will you, Lori?''

Lori chuckled, and he smothered a groan. Yeah, like that was going to happen. Who did he think he was fooling? Merely interested in Alexis? After that call, the whole town would call him a totally infatuated fool. A guy like him going after a woman like Alexis.

Yet he couldn't help himself. He'd never faced jealousy before in his life till now and he didn't know how to handle it. He'd fretted over the problem all day before going to the school to see her. Was Alexis still in love with that guy or not?

Now James glanced at his watch again. Another two minutes. Then he saw her car turn the corner and pull into the lot, and let his breath escape in a stream.

He was there to open her door. He was very attentive as he watched her lips curve into a soft smile. Yep. She could be temptation, big time.

The following night Alexis sat with Lori and Kathy, smiling all through the concert at the bright young faces filled with joy and pride as they showed off their hard work. She loved children's voices. Perhaps she should offer to help with an after-school music program. She'd probably have the time next year.

Afterward, Judy found her among the milling crowd leaving the school auditorium.

"The vests are a great success, Alexis. Lots of people have commented on how nice they are. Thanks again for all your effort. You put in more hours than anyone, and all of us appreciate it."

"I'm glad they turned out so well, Judy," she replied. Judy hurried away to find her daughter.

"Well, it's only nine o'clock," Lori mentioned, glancing at her watch. "Why don't we find something to eat somewhere?"

"I can go for that, but doesn't Steven expect you home?" Alexis asked.

"He's out of town." Lori tossed her a saucy grin. "I have the whole evening free." They pushed through the outside doors, the evening air cooling their skin. "Hmm...I have a better idea. Why don't we send out for pizza and chow down at my house? With Steven gone, we can have a hen party."

"I'm game," Kathy said. "My hubby won't mind, as long as I'm not too late."

"Sounds good to me," Alexis said. "Beats going home to an empty apartment. I'll order now, if you want. Then it won't be as long a wait."

"Okay, we're on," Lori said. "Let me catch a couple of the others."

By the time Alexis reached Lori's house, her friend had collected two other single teachers.

"Whee, am I super glad that concert is over,"

Sandy Johnson, one of the sixth-grade teachers, said as she collapsed on Lori's flowered couch. "Though I loved doing it, I'm glad it's done."

"Me, too, and I had no real part in making it happen," Lori said, handing around cans of soda. Then she lifted her glass, toasting Alexis. "As the new teacher this year, Alexis, I salute you. You've paid your dues by doing all that extra work on the kids' vests. You're one of us."

"That's very true," Kathy added. "Alexis has proven herself all year as one of the best teachers with special-needs kids," Kathy added.

"Thanks, all of you," Alexis replied, feeling the warm glow of the approval of her peers. "But we all work hard."

"Yeah, but you even handle the parents better than most," Kathy said. "Especially J. D. Sullivan."

"J.D.?" Sandy asked, her eyes wide. "I knew him in high school. He was a hunk then, and from the few times I've seen him around town, I guess he still is. I didn't realize he had a kid in school, though."

"Yes, his son Cliff came to us only recently," Alexis said. "It's been a difficult adjustment for both of them."

Alexis chewed on her pepperoni pizza and offered nothing more. Lori jumped in and explained the current situation.

"Aw, poor kid. Poor J.D." Courtney, their fifth fellow teacher, sat on the floor. "I'm sorry for them both. But," she continued, pursing her lips, "as long as J.D. is single again, I sure wish he'd cast an eye my way."

"Ha!" Sandy's eyes sparked like the fourth of July. "You aren't the only one. I wonder what excuse I could use to visit his boat shop?"

"I don't know, but I may just find one," Courtney said. "But he doesn't sell boats, does he? Too bad. I could pretend to want one for the summer."

Lori gave Alexis a twinkling gaze and raised her brows. Should she let the others in on the growing interest James had shown in Alexis?

Alexis narrowed her eyes at her friend.

"Well…" Lori said, letting her dimples show. "I think our hometown boy is already casting his line elsewhere. Say, talking about boats…"

Alexis let her breath out. She was safe from a ton of teasing for a little while longer.

Alexis hoped to sleep late the next morning, but she woke early to a snuffling dog near her bed. Poor thing, he felt neglected. "I'll make it up to you today, Pepper boy," she muttered as she pushed herself out of bed. "You won't have to stay with me too much longer. Mom will be back in a few days and you can go home."

Yet Pepper had made friends. Cliff had said good-bye five times when she picked Pepper up on Thursday night.

Neither she nor James had rushed it. They'd stood outside his house, letting the two play under the street lamp. But a school night dictated a decent bedtime, so she didn't linger, either.

Last night, the clutch of teachers at Lori's house

hadn't broken up until midnight. To her relief, most of their remaining chatter concerned the summer.

Alexis couldn't bring herself to really think about the summer months looming ahead without specific plans of her own. It was a first for her. She supposed she'd spend time with her parents and perhaps even join her sister, Eileen, on a trip to Europe.

It was the answer she used when anyone asked her, but she didn't elaborate. Instead, she steered the conversation to cover the remaining two weeks of school. She and Lori had two field trips planned, one to the Truman Museum and the other to the dam that had created the Lake of the Ozarks.

One of her tasks this Saturday morning was to co-ordinate the parent volunteers. Yawning, she stared at the cardboard box sitting on her living room floor. That remained to be sorted, too. She turned her back and reached for a can of dog food.

"C'mon, Pepper boy. Eat your breakfast and I'll take you for a walk."

She pulled on an old pair of knee-length denim shorts and a T-shirt from collage. Padding around barefoot, she nibbled at toast and coffee. When the phone rang, she snatched it up, hoping it was a return call from a mother she'd been trying to reach.

It was, but Alexis was disappointed to find the mother unable to take the day off from work for a field trip. That left her with only one helper—not enough in her opinion, especially since Kathy wasn't sure she'd be available the day they planned to go to the dam. Alexis was mulling over her problem when the phone rang again.

"I'm popular this morning, huh, boy?" she murmured, pushing her feet into sandals before answering.

"Hi, Alexis. It's Ron."

Only a few months before, the baritone on the other end of the line would have been a welcome voice. Now the only emotion that surfaced was a mild irritation.

"Oh, Ron. How are you?"

"Fine, fine. How are things with you?"

"Good." She waited a moment, then asked, "Are you calling from Dallas? How are things working out for you there?"

"Yes, I'm in Dallas. I'm quite happy I made the change, but... Say, Alexis, I'm going to be in K.C. next weekend. I'd like to see you while I'm there."

"Next weekend is impossible, Ron. It's the final week of the school year and I'll be wrapping up too much here."

"Can't you take care of all that some other time, Alexis? I'll only be in town for a couple of days."

Alexis twisted her kitchen phone cord, recalling just how rigid Ron could be. At one time, she'd have rushed to rearrange her schedule to fit his. That was part of their problem; he'd never been willing to compromise for her at all. He always expected her to bend his way.

Truthfully, she could manage to free up her weekend if she wanted to, but that was something she no longer wanted. Not for Ron. "No, I really can't, Ron. Sorry."

He hesitated. "All right. Perhaps I'll make a run down to see you on Sunday. We can at least have dinner somewhere, can't we?"

"Maybe. Would you like to come in time to attend church with me?"

"Uh, no—" he cleared his throat "—I have several things I have to do. I don't think I'll be available until nearly eleven."

No, he wouldn't be. She'd often attended church without him, even when he promised to come.

"Okay." She let it go with a mental shrug. She no longer expected more than Ron was capable of giving.

That was *her* problem. Hadn't her mom said it? Alexis had set her standards for a husband so impossibly high that only a true paragon would ever fit her criteria. Her mother doubted any man at all would fit.

"I'm not sure where I'll be in the afternoon," she said. "If you decide to come, give me a call. You have my number."

She hung up, then took Pepper's leash from the hook by the door. As she fumbled with her lock, she glanced at the untouched cardboard box. She truly did have to sort it through.

But not this morning.

Chapter Fourteen

Alexis had only one excuse to visit James at his shop today. As the parent of one of her students he could be a candidate to serve as parent supervisor on the field trip.

He wouldn't, of course. She didn't expect him to close his shop for a whole day, and she could verify that with a simple phone call—but she'd rather see him face-to-face.

She'd become addicted to seeing him, and lately she hadn't seen him nearly enough. She let out a long sigh.

The tug of attraction between them whirled ever stronger, like a stream tumbling into rapids, something to negotiate carefully. The intensity was something past her experience, and the worst of it was that it had nowhere to go. Why couldn't she simply move on, go back home to her parents' house for the summer? Forget him?

But no matter what, she still wanted to see him today. The excuse of a parent-teacher meeting would have to do in a pinch.

Alexis continued her stroll toward the business district of town, letting Pepper investigate his surroundings as they went, mulling over what she would do— should do—with her summer. She'd signed with the school district to teach another year in Sunny Creek, but perhaps transferring to a district closer to her parents next year was a wiser idea. Her aunt's fall had struck a chord in her mind, a recognition that her mom and dad were growing older. They might need her to be close by.

Alexis wrinkled her brow. For the first time in her life she felt like a real grown-up. On the other hand, she was acting like a love-struck teenager, and she'd never been that boy-crazy when she *was* a teen.

None of her decisions seemed to come easily this last year.

Heavenly Father, I don't understand this craziness, this restlessness I feel. I always knew where I was headed with my life, clearly knew what kind of future I wanted. Now… Help me to evaluate where I am going in my life, where I need to be…

Who I need to spend my life with.

She passed a store two doors down from James's shop, Bea's Flea Market, and then paused to glance unseeingly in the windows of a secondhand bookstore. Outdated history books were displayed with old journals, a pair of ancient leather gloves and a woman's hat from the nineteenth century. The items suggested a more demur time when women usually behaved with reticence.

Reserve and reticence weren't qualities that could be laid at her door. She chuckled at herself and shook off her serious mood. Only ten days left of the school year and she was going to make the most of them.

Pepper wouldn't be welcome in most stores, but since Alexis already knew James had no problem with the small dog visiting, she held the leash tightly and entered through the shop door.

The bell dinged, alerting all to her entrance. A young couple looked over a display of life jackets and other boating gear and paid her little attention.

James was with another customer. The two of them hovered over a long form. James glanced up from writing on it long enough to give her a nod, his eyes flashing a warm welcome.

"Be with you in a minute, Alexis."

"Sure."

His customer was Galen Stallings. It seemed to her she'd run into the businessman quite a lot lately. He, too, gave her a nod, but then returned his attention to the catalog they studied.

"You can finish that up later, J.D.," Galen said. "You've already called it in to the manufacturer and they've agreed to a rush order—that's what I care about. I've another stop to make in town so I can swing back to sign the order later. Meanwhile, think about what we've discussed."

"I will, Galen. And…thanks."

"Think about what?" Alexis asked before she

could check herself, her gaze following the older man as he exited the shop.

She brought herself up short. It was a nosy question, and she wasn't entitled to ask it. She wasn't in the classroom now.

Then, realizing her student was nowhere in sight, she asked, "Where's Cliff this morning?"

James, who had thoughtfully watched Galen out of sight, turned to her.

"Cliff is with Robby. His folks and I have traded time slots. Cliff is spending the day with Robby, and Robby is spending the night with Cliff so his folks can have an evening to themselves. I promised them pizza for supper." He let a grin spread. "Want to join us?"

"Uh, maybe." A responsive smile tugged at her lips.

Maybe?

He leaned his arms on the glass counter and said just above a whisper, "Could I turn that 'maybe' to a definite 'yes' if we were to have Tina sit with the boys later on so we could take in a movie? Or even a stroll?"

His low tone warmed her, courted her. An evening saunter with James? The May evenings were balmy and it should be a clear night. Did he honestly think she'd refuse?

"A stroll? A 'yes' is definitely a possibility...."

He broke away as the young couple brought their choices to the counter. James rung up their purchases and the two exited, leaving the shop empty of customers.

"What can I do for you this morning, Teach?" he said then. "After your late night with the girls after the concert, you surely didn't come in here to find Cliff."

She wrinkled her brow. "The grapevine already?"

"Don't worry about it," he said with a wink. "I had reason to talk with Lori this morning. She wants to find out more about a building project of Galen's."

Alexis wandered to the huge map of central Missouri on the far wall. Details of the Lake of the Ozarks, Truman Lake and Pomme de Terre showed more inlets, channels, ridges and curvy roads than she'd dreamed were there. She sought out the dam, following with her finger the route they'd drive. She hadn't visited Bagnell Dam in years, not since she was a child.

"So, are you looking for Cliff?" James said, coming up behind her. "Or me?"

His voice was an invitation, sending a tingling up her spine. "You, I guess. Uh, I, uh, do have a bit of a quandary."

"Seems to me those pesky little predicaments follow you around," he teased.

"Not at all, I…I merely have problems to solve like everyone."

"Face it, Alexis, you thrive on puzzles and problems. You're a fixer. Like me."

"A fixer?"

"Yep. Only, we like fixing different things."

She wondered where he was taking this conversation. "How do you figure that?"

"Easy. I like repairing things." He shoved his hands in his back pockets. "At least with things, there's a concrete end. You can either repair something—or not. If a thing is really worn out or too old to get parts, the answer is simple. You junk it and replace it with something new. A finish, an end of the problem.

"Now people…" His stare became contemplative. "You like helping people, but they're never finished, are they? Sometimes they aren't fixable either. But just as the scripture says…God doesn't throw any of us away. We can junk ourselves, but God doesn't do it. He gives us that choice—we can take His offer and become new or head for the junk pile."

The phone rang, and Alexis stood stunned at the depth of James's understanding as he left her side to answer it. He'd really thought about this. Mending things, mending people…

Perhaps he *had* tagged her correctly. Why else would she have entered the field she had? Teaching children with behavior disorders as well as other disabilities was a difficult career. And one of the most satisfying. Her field took her to the edge and back. For her, the victories and accomplishments came in small increments, but each achievement with a student always gave her a high. Her pride rode high as well. She'd worked hard to be the best, and knew she was good at her job.

Yet a feeling of inadequacy plagued her at times.

For all her continuing education, practical solutions and hard work, she realized some youngsters couldn't be "fixed." That often left her in tears. In those moments she turned to God, praying earnestly for her students. And for herself. Nothing could be achieved, she knew, if God didn't guide and bless her efforts.

"So, what do you need this morning? What's your problem?"

Caught deep in thought, Alexis was startled when he returned to her side, but she had to admit he'd gone straight to it.

"Um…all right, you win," she said, and smiled. "I do need something. Lori and I are coming up short on parents to go with us on our field trip to Bagnell Dam. We need parents for the trip up to the Truman Library, too. I don't suppose there is any way you could volunteer?"

"Hmm… Are you sure you want *me?* You know I don't have the patience you do. I don't put up with as much kid nonsense as you."

"True, but in this case that's not all bad. A father with a strong voice on one of these trips is always a plus. The kids respond to a male voice much better, so keeping them in line is easier."

"A strong voice, huh," he said, his tone rife with teasing. "Why didn't that work with you a couple of weeks ago?"

"I did listen," she replied with indignity. "But I lost my balance."

"Excuses, excuses…"

"Well, I told you I wasn't a fisherman."

"Yeah, yeah. Well, you'll have to learn more about boat safety, too."

"If I promise to pay better attention to those safety rules, will you come?"

"I'm not so sure I'm a good candidate for a field trip."

"I think you're perfect for such an outing."

He studied her face with a sudden intensity, making her wonder what he was thinking.

"You're sure?"

"Yes. If you could manage it, I'm sure."

"Okay." A soft light shone in his brown gaze. "Give me a day or two and I'll see what I can do."

"Really?" His response sent pleasure through her. "That would be terrific, James."

"Why can't we go skateboarding?" Cliff begged that evening as he watched a pair of teens indulging their sport on the otherwise empty tennis court.

Remnants of pizza, paper plates and sodas littered the picnic table at the local park, where they'd taken their carryout meal. The twenty rolling acres sat next to the local golf club, with houses on large lots surrounding the course.

Tina had promised to meet them at seven-thirty, and it was almost that now.

"You and Robby have been active all day," J.D. answered firmly. He leaned back in his lawn chair, relaxed and content with listening to bird calls, watching the boys run and waving away flies. For the moment.

"But Dad…"

"You spent the whole afternoon at the pool. It's time to settle down for the night."

"I don't want to go home." Cliff pushed out his chin. "It's not even dark."

"It will be dark soon enough." James glanced at Alexis. Her hair lay smoothly brushed to reach just past her shoulders, and he recalled how silky it felt to his touch. He liked the feel of it.

His pulse quickened. Having her in his life was becoming a habit. The day he'd taken her home soaking wet, her hair darkened, both of them still chuckling over her fishing adventure, hung in his mind. He'd earnestly wished as he'd dropped her off at her apartment that they could go home together. Once planted, that thought had hooked him well. He'd been angling for more time together every day since, but was too often thwarted.

Starting tonight, he planned to do all he could to correct that problem. If her summer plans included staying in town…

He feared she'd leave town for the summer. What if the contents of that box mattered more to her than Lori thought? What if she didn't come back to Sunny Creek next year in spite of everything? What if her former boyfriend wanted her back? What if she still loved that guy?

What if she is only flirting with me? Filling time until she can work things out with what's-his-name?

"But I never get to skateboard anymore." Cliff wasn't ready to give up his argument. "You're always working and there's no good place at home. Here there's a parking lot.''

"I'll bring you over tomorrow afternoon for a while," James promised. He silently admitted his son's complaint was true enough. He hadn't wedged in time to indulge his son's passion.

"We can build a ramp in my backyard," Robby, blue-eyed and angelic looking, suggested. "There's one over in Kirk's neighborhood. It's big, and—"

"Who's Kirk?" Alexis asked, directing her question toward James's with an amused smile. She busied herself by gathering up the trash.

James shrugged. "I don't know everyone in town."

"I rather thought you did," she answered with a chuckle.

Tina arrived and the boys greeted her with some excitement. "Tina, can we go see Kirk's skate ramp?" Robby asked.

After a quick glance at James, Tina said, "Um, not tonight, guys. How about a video game challenge until bedtime?"

"Thanks, Tina. We won't be too late." James handed her his house key. It didn't take long for Tina to round up the two boys and cart them home.

"Tina is good with the boys," Alexis commented.

"Yes, she is. Lucky for me."

"I wonder if she has considered becoming a teacher."

James didn't know what their young friend's ambitions were, but he knew Alexis had a deep curiosity about other people.

"Don't know. Maybe you should ask her."

Ask... Simple enough if a guy wanted to know something. He still wanted to know about the contents of that big cardboard box he'd carried for Alexis. Lori's evaluation wasn't enough. He wanted to hear from Alexis herself.

James made sure their litter was deposited in the trash can. Then he reached for her hand, wrapping her soft fingers in his.

They strolled past a handful of teens playing baseball as the last hour of sunlight brushed the park in evening golds and blue shadows. Eventually they returned to the truck. He helped her into it and drove along the drive that led to the highest ridge of the region.

"There's an overlook up here that's pretty awesome," he said, steering toward a rising semicircle. He braked and turned off the motor. The area, framed in sky-reaching hardwood trees, opened on one side to rolling hills and valleys below. Crickets and other night creatures began their chorus. "Have you been here yet?"

"Actually, I have," she answered. "When I came down to Sunny Creek to interview last year, and again last fall. It is one of the town's best assets."

He got out and went around to her side just in time to let her slide out and into his arms.

It was too good to miss. He held her close and found her lips with his. They were warm and velvet soft. He felt lost in the sweet fragrance of her, the feel of her, and felt lost as their breaths mingled.

A car announced its arrival with blaring rap music and a passenger's snide catcall. He ignored the teen couple, and slowly let her go, suggesting, "Let's go see the view."

Below them lay a series of tree-covered ridges and valleys, and the darkening blue lake in the distance. Growing shadows hid many of the homes, resorts and boat marinas dotting the miles of shoreline, but white wake followed a few die-hard boaters.

"It looks too perfect to be true," Alexis murmured. She sank to sit on the low stone wall that lined the perimeter. "A picture postcard of paradise."

"Uh-huh. I'd warrant there's not many places any better or prettier," he said with pride as he gazed into the distance. He stood close, feeling the brush of her shoulder against his thighs.

"I could stay here till dawn," she said dreamily.

Then he laughed and slapped the side of his neck. "Except this piece of paradise has flies and mosquitoes."

"Do you want to go, then?"

"No. I want to…" He bent, sliding his fingers under her chin as he kissed her again.

"Hey, dude!" came a young male voice from another arriving car. "Smoky's on his way up here. Patrols are tight on weekends."

"We'd better go," Alexis murmured. He thought he heard regret in her voice. "We seem to have invaded the teen make-out point."

"Okay. But I do have something I need to ask you. Can we talk at your place?"

Chapter Fifteen

They heard a fire siren begin to wail as they left the scenic drive. The mournful sound grew louder, more demanding as they drove toward town. James switched on his two-way radio. The dispatcher's disembodied voice sounded cool but urgent.

"...believed to be the line of shops..."

He frowned and turned up the volume.

"Are you on call?" Alexis asked as James leaned forward. Sunny Creek had been lucky this spring. The town had had only one quickly extinguished backyard brush fire to challenge the firefighters and their new fire truck. To her knowledge, there had been no other emergencies in their town all spring.

"No, but this sounds—"

"...on Fifth and Main..."

James's mouth tightened and he abruptly stomped on the gas pedal. "Tighten your seat belt and brace yourself," he commanded, his hand closing on the steering wheel like a vise. Around them, traffic increased. He leaned on the horn, calculating his speed with care as they dodged in and around other vehicles.

They smelled smoke long before they saw flames. The street was choked with vehicles and people. James guided his truck to a skidding stop half a block away from Sullivan's Repair. Beyond, the street was blocked by county sheriff department cars in addition to Sunny Creek's own two.

Yanking at his seat belt clasp, James shoved open his door and dropped to the street. "Catch up to you later," he tossed over his shoulder as he raced away.

Alexis followed at a lope, pushing her way through the growing crowd that was observing the fire and firefighters from across the street. A uniformed officer with the sheriff's department worked at crowd control, and an ambulance waited nearby. She didn't know where James had disappeared to, but she spotted Lori and her husband Steven in the crowd. She went to stand beside them.

"Hi, Lori. Steven," she greeted, trying to gauge how widespread the fire was. The only flames she could actually see were from the south end of the line, yet the heat and smoke poured into the air. It was hard to determine just where the fire raged hottest. A pumper truck streamed water into the center, but men swarmed everywhere.

"What happened? Which shop is on fire?"

"They think it started in the flea market, but no one's sure," Lori answered. "But it has spread along the shared roofline."

"Oh, no. Are all the shops burning?" Alexis asked frantically. Smoke-filled air made her choke. She barely glanced about her, not caring who else was nearby. Horror and fascination kept her gaze glued on the action.

She felt her tummy churn. Where was James? Surely he hadn't gone into the building?

"Don't know about all of 'em, yet," Steven said. "But none are getting off without damage even when they get it under control. Saw James go by."

"Where is he?"

"I saw him talking to Jackson Carrick, the fire chief, a minute ago," Lori told her, as Steven sidled his way closer to the fire trucks. "Denny is here, too. The two of them just geared up."

"Geared up?" Alarm crawled up her spine like an unwelcome insect. "You mean he's going into the fire?"

"Both James and Denny have fought fires before, Alexis." Lori flashed her a knowing glance, then assured almost too brightly, "They know what they're doing."

Then, under her breath, Lori finished her thought. "When they're not acting as daredevils."

"Thanks a lot, Lori," Alexis muttered, her teeth clinched. "You're a big help."

"I knew it!" Lori crowed. "You're hooked on J.D."

"Lori! Just because we've been seeing each other a bit doesn't mean…"

Then she felt her heart sink even further. Who was

she fooling? *It's true. I am hook, line, sinker and over-my-head gaga about James Dean Sullivan. What a disaster.*

"This is where J.D.'s shop is, isn't it?" Steven asked as he returned. "He's in the middle there, isn't he?"

It took a minute for Alexis to gather her wits to answer. "Uh-huh. Sullivan's Repair occupies that third store space—" Alexis nodded toward it "—next to Hildebrand's Insurance."

She felt her heart sink as she realized what this would do to James's business. All the businesses...

"Thank God it's a Saturday night when all the shops along here are closed," Alexis heard someone behind them say. "They don't stay open late like the new stores out on the highway."

"Yeah, usually they are closed by this time of night," Lori muttered as she leaned over to speak in Alexis's ear. "But lights were on in the back of the bookstore. More than just the security lights. The woman that owns it might have been there."

"No one was there, Lori," Steven said, frowning at his wife. "Don't go making something out of nothing."

"Well, I'm only reporting what was seen," Lori insisted.

Shattering glass riveted their attention, and Alexis heard "ooh" and "look at that" around her. Then she realized the front plate window in Sullivan's Repair had broken. Shards lay all over the sidewalk in front. The shouting activity increased when a county fire truck arrived to help. Commands came from one of the officers. "Move away, folks. Move back."

Shifting with the crowd, Alexis stood on her toes to see better. She spotted James in the thick of it, and held her breath. Then she lost sight of him as he disappeared to the rear of the shops with two other men.

Lord, please keep James safe from harm. Keep them all safe.

"Well, what's old sour face doing here?" she heard Lori say.

Alexis turned to see who her friend meant. "Who?"

"There." Lori nodded toward their school superintendent, talking with Jackson Carrick. His dark summer suit hung on his sharp, puppet-like bones, his long skinny neck revealed by an open shirt collar. He moved with jerky awkwardness.

"Fisher? What about him?"

"I never would have figured him for a siren chaser, would you?"

"No, I wouldn't," Alexis agreed, watching the man's agitation. "He's in his usual uproar, I see. Why do you suppose he is so upset now?"

"Who knows," Lori replied with a shrug.

Extinguishing the fire seemed to take many hours, when in fact it took less than two. The rising smoke continued to throw a polluting odor into the air, shrouding the joined buildings from the street lamps and screening out what little moonlight the night afforded.

The crowd began to drift away, but Alexis didn't

move. She couldn't leave until she knew how James had fared. Knew that he was unharmed. Knew how much damage his shop had sustained.

"Poor J.D.," Lori murmured. "This is a low blow just when his summer season has started. And the others. They depend a lot on summer trade."

"Yes, it'll hurt business, sure enough—if not close it down completely," Steven added.

James held a mountain of pride in his shop. He'd talked on occasion about his years of building it. What would he do now? *Lord, let the insurance be sufficient....*

He broke away from a threesome of firefighters, then, and Alexis noticed that his gaze searched the crowd. Was he looking for her? Did he need her? *Lord, I only hope so.*

She stepped away from the people around her. "James."

He came straight toward her. His face streaked with soot, his eyes looked bleak. He started to reach for her hand, then dropped his.

"Alexis, can you find your own way home?" He glanced at Lori and Steven. Dennis Bender, his sandy hair above sober blue-gray eyes that never missed a jot, lingered beside them.

James didn't bother to introduce him.

"Yes, I suppose, but—" She wanted to touch James's face, to brush away some of the shadows in his eyes. She felt dreadful for him, knowing he hid his anguish at seeing his business destroyed.

"Good. Then, please do me a favor." His voice was

tight. "Call Tina and ask her to spend the night with the boys. Or maybe you'd better phone Robby's parents. They might prefer to come pick up Robby under the circumstances. If that's the case, then Tina can stay with Cliff. Then you go on home."

"I want to stay here, James. Perhaps there's something—"

"Don't talk nonsense, Alexis. This place won't be safe for anyone to poke around in for hours, but I'm not leaving until we can secure the site."

"Is that necessary?"

"Yes. Very necessary," Denny said as he joined the conversation. "We don't know exactly how the fire started, and there's always a chance it may break out again."

"Oh. Well, I guess... How will you do that?" she asked James. "Secure the area?"

It seemed to her an almost impossible task. The six shops covered much of the city block.

"Denny and I will patrol the place until morning."

"Good idea," Steven put in. "Our police force of one is out of town and there is always the possibility of looters."

"Looters?" Alexis heart nearly jumped into her throat. Couldn't that be dangerous? "I hadn't even thought of that."

"Oh, my stars!" Lori said, her eyes wide.

"Nice work, Steven. Scare the women, why don't you?" Denny said.

"No, I'm not frightened," Alexis insisted. She wouldn't admit it even if it were true. And it wasn't true…she wouldn't allow it to be. "I trust that James knows what he is doing."

She stood straighter and touched James's arm. "Don't worry about the boys. I'll make sure they're fine and stay with them. There's no need to wake them tonight."

A call from the fire chief broke into the conversation.

"Thanks, Alexis," James murmured, and hurried away with Denny in tow.

Lori and Steven dropped her at James's place. Tina let her in, and Alexis quickly explained what happened.

Then, for the first time, she gazed around at the tiny house, cramped and cluttered. Alexis checked on Cliff and Robby, sprawled out in sleeping bags on the living room floor. Pepper, curled against Cliff, rose to greet her; idly, she bent down to pet him. She and Tina spoke in whispers as she answered the girl's questions.

"That old string of shops has been there all my life," Tina said, her hand covering her mouth in horror over the destruction Alexis described. "I know Mrs. Shoemaker who has the flea market and J.D. and some of the others. What will they all do now?"

"I don't know, Tina. I guess it depends on how much the insurance will cover and what the owner decides to do with the property. I'm sure that James will be all right eventually. After all, most of his business is based on a service rather than only product."

Alexis prayed it was true. James would recover, but

where? And what of all the other businesses? It was a tragedy.

She sent Tina home, then pulled out her cell phone and turned it on; someone aside from James might need to call her.

Then she switched off all but a single low lamp and settled down on the couch. She pillowed her head in her arms, smelling the smoke on her skin. Wow, what she wouldn't give for a hot shower, she mused, knowing it had to wait until morning. The thought drifted from her mind as she thought of the long night ahead; James and Denny patrolling the fire zone, hopefully with others helping.

Lord, please send strength to James and Denny tonight. They need help.

She slept fitfully and rose well before six, moving quietly so as not to wake the boys. Searching the cabinets, she found instant coffee and made herself a cup. At seven, she found the number for Robby's parents and called them, explaining what had happened. They promised to pick up their son in twenty minutes.

When her cell phone rang, she jumped and dived for her purse.

"Hello."

"Alexis?" Ron answered, his tone irritated. "I've been trying to reach you. Why haven't you returned my call?"

"Oh, Ron." Disappointment that it wasn't James shot through her. "I haven't had time."

The boys stirred. Cliff blinked at her, then sat up. He frowned, his brown eyes growing worried. "Miss

Richmond. What are you doing here? Where's my dad?''

Alexis covered the mouthpiece and spoke calmly. ''He's taking care of a problem down at the shop, Cliff. We'll hear from him sometime this morning. Meantime, you boys get dressed. Robby, your parents will be here shortly to pick you up.''

In her ear, Ron demanded, ''What do you mean by that? You didn't have time? You knew I was in town for only the weekend and I waited all day yesterday for you to call.''

''Sorry, Ron. I didn't realize you thought it was important.''

''I don't believe this. Alexis, this isn't like you not to call me. What's happened to you? Ever since you moved down to that little town you seem to have lost your perspective.''

''Ron, I really would like to hear another analysis of what's wrong with my personality,'' she said, realizing she'd heard his critical opinion once too often, ''but I don't have time for it. I've been dealing with an emergency situation and I have to go now.''

''Wait. Alexis…what emergency?''

''A local situation. Nothing that affects me, but…''

What a fib, she thought. It affected her in ways she had yet to think about, but she wasn't about to try figuring it all out now. Her mind was too fuzzy from lack of sleep.

''Alexis, I miss you.''

A few months ago that admission would have sent her to pack a bag and fill her gas tank. Now it had little effect except to make her wonder if she'd ever been in love with Ron at all. "What about today? I don't fly out until tomorrow morning. Can't you drive home today?"

A solid rapping on the door sent her across the living room.

"Ron, it's impossible. I'm needed here. Maybe next time you're in town? I can't talk any longer. Goodbye." She disconnected her phone and let Robby's parents in.

Thirty minutes later, James came home just as Alexis was preparing to take Cliff to church. Soot caked his skin, and the odor of smoke wafted in his wake. He stood just inside the door, touching nothing.

"Is the fire totally out?" she asked, letting her gaze rove over him, assuring herself he was unhurt.

"Yeah." His voice burred with exhaustion. "All the store owners are there—starting to sift through the rubble as it cools to see what can be recovered. Investigators, too."

"Investigators?"

"Yeah. All kinds. Police, fire and insurance. So far we think the fire started at the flea market, but we won't know for sure for some hours."

"Dad, did you fight that fire?" Cliff asked, a dawning hero worship in his gaze. He scrambled off his kitchen stool where he'd been munching toast.

"Yeah, son. Me and Uncle Denny and some others." Then he cautioned, "Don't get too close to me. I'm filthy."

"Did you get burned?" Cliff's wonder and anxiety

swirled into a what-could-have-been, and he frowned with worry. "You look like it."

"Look that bad, do I?" James glanced down at himself, then at Cliff. His gaze shimmered with love and understanding of the boy's new concern. "No, son, I wasn't burned."

"How bad is the loss?" Alexis asked. Her heart ached for him, for all the years of twelve- and four-teen-hour days and more he sometimes spent in build-ing an independent business.

"Pretty bad for some. Not so bad for our end, but bad enough."

"James, you're exhausted. Have a shower and I'll make you some breakfast."

"Can't stay," he said, his gaze bleak. "Came home only to see how you're making out with Cliff." He rubbed between his eyes with a thumb. "Hate to ask it, Alexis, but could you look after Cliff for the day?"

"Don't worry about Cliff, James. We'll go on to church and then he can stay with me," she said. In spite of his condition, she reached out to touch his cheek. "But you need some nutrition."

He shook his head. "Maybe later. The Pancake House sent food over about an hour ago. Couldn't eat. Coffee would be good, though."

She moved into the kitchenette and turned on the coil beneath the pot of water. Then she spooned coffee granules into a mug. "Is it really necessary for you to go back?"

"Haven't had any phone calls here, have I?" He asked without replying to her question.

"No."

"Miss Richmond, you had a phone call," Cliff reminded. "Don't you remember?"

Alexis looked up from pouring hot water into the mug. "Yes, Cliff, but that wasn't for your dad."

"It was some guy named Ron," Cliff said helpfully.

James glanced at her, his eyes giving nothing of his feelings away. Then he gave a curt nod. "Okay. Gotta go, now. I'll keep in touch...."

He left without his coffee.

Chapter Sixteen

The fire was all the talk at church that morning. Alexis guessed it was probably the only subject in town. Such a big fire was a loss to a town their size. Noting Cliff by her side without James, a number of people expressed their condolences toward the boy. They asked Alexis to take messages and offers of help along to J.D.

Cliff, more restless than usual, could barely sit still throughout the service, so as soon as it ended, Alexis drove the few blocks to the center of town. The boy would feel calmer if he saw for himself what had happened.

Motor traffic was still barricaded for a couple of blocks on either side of the old strip mall. She parked as close as she could, and they walked the remainder of the way.

The place swarmed with gapers. People milled

about or stood staring from behind the plastic tape that served as an official barrier.

In daylight, the remains of broken walls and charred, ashy rubble looked every bit as dreadful as Alexis had feared. Although the brick walls stood, the roof was intact for only a few feet on either end. All six shops were damaged to various degrees, but only two were totally destroyed—Bea's Flea Market and Hildebrand's Insurance, next to Sullivan's Repair.

She spotted Denny and James standing with two men in uniform near James's broken window. Denny talked, and James shook his head—a sorrowful gesture, Alexis thought. A slight frown settled on his brow, his mouth in a grim line, James looked more discouraged than Alexis had ever seen him.

Helplessness hit her with an uncomfortable depth of feeling. The horrible shock of it left her totally vulnerable. This disaster was beyond anything she could do to help.

Cliff broke away from her and ran ahead. "Dad!"

James glanced up, then strode to meet them, straightening his shoulders as he came as though throwing off his discouragement.

"Stay there, Cliff. Don't cross the barrier."

Cliff obeyed, but strained to see.

"He wasn't going to be happy until he came to see what happened," she explained. "Actually, I wanted to come, too. But we won't stay for long."

"It's okay," he said. "Suppose I should've expected it. I'd have been just as antsy at his age. At any age, I guess."

"Did it burn everything?" Cliff asked.

"Pretty much, Cliff."

"Did my catalogs burn, too?"

"Yeah, son. Sorry. But we can get new product catalogs."

"That's good. What about the other stuff?" The boy hopped on one foot, then another. "The props and oars and that stuff?"

"Reckon we can recover some of it." James didn't sound very positive, and Alexis thought the effects of the whole disaster must be catching up to him. The afternoon sun beat down with an unusual heat for May. Sweat drops rolled down James's cheeks. Tired lines were etched around his eyes and deep grooves bracketed his mouth.

"What's going to happen now?" she asked. She wanted to cry for him, wanted to touch him with reassurance. There was so little she could say in the face of his loss.

"Well, all of us have renters' insurance. But the building…" He shook his head. He glanced over his shoulder toward the knot of men. "No one knows what will happen yet. We're going to decide that in a day or two. After we reach the owner."

"Where is he?" she asked. Her empathy welled higher. James appeared calm and collected about the disaster, but behind his brown eyes lay an uncertainty. The others must feel it, too, she thought.

"We're not sure. Would you believe it? This strip mall is insured by Hildebrand's Insurance there—" he pointed over his shoulder with a thumb "—and now their records are gone."

"Who owns it?"

"A man named Lennox. He used to be around a couple of times a year, but not this past year at all. The insurance agent hasn't been able to find him yet. He's been mostly an absentee landlord for the past few years. Lives some of his year down in Florida."

"Is that why you've had so much trouble getting repairs?"

"Yeah, that's part of it. The other part of it is he's just tight with a buck." He rubbed the spot between his eyes with his thumb. "But nothing more can be done here until we talk to him."

"Well, Caroline and Fitz said they'll help clean up if you need them," Alexis told James. "And others at church made offers, too."

"That's nice." He nodded, then, as though deciding he needed to add something, he mumbled, "Real nice."

"Dad, can I go look for that box with the tools in it?"

"No, Cliff, you can't go in there at all. It's still too hot, you'd get burned."

"But I'd be careful."

"I said no, Cliff, and I mean it. You hear?" James gave her a desperate glance, then mumbled, "That would be a real nightmare."

"After your dad gets matters sorted out, perhaps you can help him put it all in order again," she said, placing a hand on the boy's shoulder.

Gazing at James, she thought her heart would turn over. She fought the knot in her throat as she tried to speak. "I'll keep Cliff with me for the rest of the day while you take care of whatever else you need to do here. But please get some sleep if you can, will you?"

A faint smile touched his lips. "Rest? Sleep? What's that? Can you give me a dictionary meaning?"

"I can have one ready for you later this afternoon," she said, shakily returning his smile in an attempt to lighten his mood. "But you need to indulge in that activity first."

"Can't promise anything today, Alexis. But I guess there's one interesting promise that will come out of this…"

"What's that?"

"I'll have the freedom to go on your field trips next week. Both of them."

Alexis nodded, then turned quickly, before her sympathetic tears spilled over to embarrass him.

Alexis and Cliff met with Lori and Steven for lunch. They kept their conversation neutral so as not to alarm the boy, and then Alexis took Cliff to her apartment. She'd dropped Pepper off and turned on her air-conditioning window unit before church. Now it whirred, and she stepped into the cooler air with gratitude.

Pepper shuffled forward to greet them, looking for company after a long quiet morning alone. Thank God for small favors, Alexis thought as Cliff folded himself down on the floor to play with him. She got out a *Peter Pan* video to help entertain him. She found pretzels for snacks, put fresh water out for Pepper, and heated water for tea. Then she settled to fill out year-end school forms.

Yet her mind often wandered. Beyond this current crisis, something else was going on with James. Yesterday, he'd wanted to talk to her. Something in his gaze had been bright with promise....

James climbed into his truck and simply sat for long, contemplative moments. He ached with exhaustion and exertion, and sported a scorched hand. Denny had gone home to his parents' house hours ago. Other volunteers kept watch over the fire scene, and there was nothing more James could do until they could truly sort through what was salvageable.

What came next? For him, for his neighbors? There had been several times in his life when he'd faced a crossroads, but he usually knew what would follow after making a decision. He didn't worry for himself; his insurance policy was in his safety deposit box in the bank. He felt grateful he'd been smart enough to have the coverage. First thing in the morning, he'd be there to collect his paperwork and follow through.

The other mall renters would be okay as far as their individual insurance payouts went. As for the future— finding another rental space as inexpensive as what the old building provided would be a real challenge. Some of his neighbors were done for.

A niggling thought had been running through his mind all morning. The building had been cheap to rent because it was old and lacking repairs or updates. But the town had grown in the past five years, and the land and location were valuable. More valuable, in fact, than when he'd moved into his space four years back.

Worth more, maybe, without the old buildings? Would the owner rebuild or sell the land?

Ah, but rebuilt, the building's rents were likely to skyrocket.

He had joined the other tenants in resisting rent increases. They had taken their protests of deteriorating conditions as far as they could, threatening to withhold rents until some repair was done. Their absentee landlord answered with a threat of eviction. They'd been at a stalemate.

So what now?

James started his motor and put the truck in gear. He wanted a shower and change before picking up Cliff. Sleep could wait. He couldn't take further advantage of Alexis. It wasn't fair to her.

It wasn't fair to subject her to all his ramblings, either, yet a part of his tired mind hoped to do just that. She had a knack for listening with patience. She knew how to point out new directions for his thinking without making him feel stupid. She offered a sweetness and strength that he'd drawn on in regard to his son. It felt natural to seek her opinions about...

His life sure had changed. His head had been turned all the way around this spring. He didn't feel as alone as he used to do, and he kind of liked it.

What would Alexis think about the choices he

faced? He could put his business back together, and he could even see his way to making it better after moving to different facilities. Expanding it. Perhaps seriously pursuing his improvement on the four-stroke motor.

Could he sell his idea to one of the big companies? Make a bit of money from it? Would that be enough to offer a woman like Alexis?

He climbed the back stairs to her apartment hoping to find a cold glass of tea and a few moments with her before taking his son home.

He knocked, listening to the soft sounds of a video over the noise of the air conditioner. The afternoon was warm, and the attic apartment would be boiling without it.

Cliff opened the door. "Hi, Dad. Can we have pizza for supper?"

"You had pizza yesterday," James reminded his son. Cliff's request would have irritated him only weeks ago. Now it seemed automatic to simply say no and offer something else. "Let's get a take-home chicken bucket."

A tall, slender man rose from Alexis's love seat as James stepped through the door. Dressed in linen summer shorts and a name-brand sports shirt, he pushed up his glasses and gazed at James with mild curiosity.

"Oh, James. Come in, please."

Alexis's gaze met his with an imploring mixture of emotions that he couldn't read.

Her lashes fluttered and she moistened her lips, then turned to introduce the stranger. "James, this is, um, a friend of mine. He drove down from Kansas City to visit for a few hours. Ron Douglas.''

Something inside him went still. That guy. The man whose ring she didn't wear but whose pictures she'd kept. The guy whom she'd been hooked up with before spring break. The boyfriend with whom she'd examined wedding invitations.

James let down his shutters. When had they gotten together again? He felt blindsided. Shut out. Why hadn't she warned him?

Maybe she hadn't wanted him to know.

Maybe those few kisses between them had meant nothing.

''Nice to meet you,'' Ron said, offering his hand to shake. ''Tough luck about the big fire.''

James slowly reached out to shake hands and said, ''J. D. Sullivan. And, thanks.''

He glanced at Alexis. She was back to being someone he barely knew. His son's teacher, a woman of compassion who only wanted to help…but who was out of his social league.

Exhaustion suddenly hit him like a tornado blast. He made a grab for politeness. ''Well, I'll take Cliff off your hands now. Thanks for all your help, Alexis. We really appreciate it—don't we, son?''

''James, let me get you some iced tea.''

''No, don't bother. I can't stay.'' He fixed his gaze on Cliff. ''C'mon, son, let's get going. Tomorrow's school and I need to get to bed.''

''I'll…I'll pick up Cliff for school tomorrow morning, James. You can sleep late for a change.''

''Thanks, but no.'' He couldn't look at her, and

turned for the door. "I have too much to do and you have your own day to work out. So long now."

So long.... It felt more like goodbye.

"Alexis, can we meet before school this morning?" Lori's tone was brisk. It was Monday morning, and Alexis sat on the side of her bed, holding the phone, blinking against her sluggishness. The morning was dark with rain, diminishing the daylight that normally streamed through her bedroom window.

For the second night in a row she had slept poorly. She hadn't convinced Ron to depart until almost midnight, leaving her to wonder if the man had always been so dense or if she'd only lately become aware of that.

It had been too late to call James.

He'd been hurt. The wounded look in his eyes as he left yesterday haunted her all night. Alexis didn't know how she was going to explain the situation, but at the first opportunity, she knew she must. If they had any chance on this earth of building on their budding relationship, she had to take a leap of faith and talk to James.

She had to tell him how she felt—that, shocking as it may seem, she was in love with him.

"Alexis?" Lori's voice jogged her.

"I suppose we can meet." Alexis pushed her hair away from her face. "What's up?"

"I'd rather wait until I see you, but do I ever have something—" Alexis heard Steven mumble something in the background, then Lori said, "Just meet me. But not at school, okay?"

"All right." A sense of intrigue captured Alexis. "Where?"

"The Pancake House in thirty minutes."

Alexis disconnected the phone call, then rushed to turn on the cold water and step under her shower. She made it quick, and afterward simply combed through her wet hair and dressed. She gathered her school papers and scattered thoughts together, then ran down her stairs and out the door.

Lori was at the restaurant before her, her small plump body vibrating with excitement.

"What's going on?" Alexis asked as she slipped into the back booth across from her friend, setting her folded umbrella aside. Even as she asked, James and Denny arrived.

James paused inside the door and removed his rain-soaked ball cap, wiping his wet face with his sleeve. Denny led the way.

When he spotted Alexis, his step faltered. Alexis's heart clamped tight. Didn't he want to see her? He let his gaze skitter away, and he slid into the booth across from her, next to Lori, leaving Denny to sit beside her.

Alexis bit into her bottom lip. Wasn't he even going to give her a chance?

"Where's Cliff?" she asked.

"Mrs. Shoemaker is taking Cliff to school this morning," James said very neutrally. "Nice lady. She's feeding him breakfast, too."

"Really good to see you, Lori," Denny said, his eyes shining with the curiosity of an old boyfriend. "You're looking great. How's Steven?"

"He's fine," Lori replied, lifting her chin. "He'd have come except he hadn't the time."

The waitress arrived with the coffeepot ready. Alexis and Lori both ordered bagels, knowing they'd have to make a quick exit to be on time for school.

"Okay." Denny shrugged. "So, what's up with this urgent call for a meeting?"

"Steven and I saw something yesterday that... Well, I think it looked a little funny, so I thought you all should hear it. Then, if you think it's anything, um, suspicious, you can take the information to Lewis Price at the police station."

"All right, what have you got?" James asked.

"Yesterday—last night, really—Steven and I ran over to Sedalia to see his parents and do a little shopping. We stopped at that drugstore on the edge of town, and Mr. Fisher was there."

"So?" Denny said.

"So he was using the public telephone. Don't you think that was strange? People seldom use public phones anymore—everyone I know has a cell phone."

"Well, it's a little strange, I guess," Alexis said, picking up her cup, "but there could be a dozen explanations. Maybe his cell phone wasn't working."

"Yeah, but I spotted him as I walked by, and when he saw me, he sorta ducked. Hunched his shoulders and turned his back."

"Lori, that still doesn't say anything significant. What are you getting at?" James asked.

"Well, I was curious, so I circled back out of sight and watched him. He sure acted cautious when he hung up, glancing around to see who was close by, then hurrying away. And folks...he was *smirking!*"

"Smirking?" Alexis repeated, raising a brow.

"Uh-huh. For Fisher, that's what passes as smiling."

Alexis stared into her cup, letting a frown form. "Uh, Lori...while it's true we've never seen Fisher smile or behave as though content with anything going on in the school district, that doesn't mean he never smiles."

Denny turned to James, pointing a thumb at Lori. "Do you know what the woman is babbling about?"

"Getting an idea, I think." James's attention was caught, and he glanced at Lori, then Alexis. "He was there at the fire scene, wasn't he? Did either of you see him?"

"Yes," Alexis said. "He was agitated, talking with the fire chief, Jackson Carrick. Stuck around for rather a long time, now that I think of it. I wouldn't have thought Mr. Fisher a thrill-seeker."

"See?" Lori practically crowed. "That kind of thing doesn't fit with his usual behavior. There's more going on inside that man's head than simply school re-districting. He's a schemer. He's a control freak. And he's up to something."

"You don't think he was at the fire out of mere curiosity?" James asked.

"Not a chance."

James looked to Alexis for confirmation.

"I don't know the man that well, James." Alexis shrugged. "You three are the homegrown talent. But I do know he is...difficult to work with and mistrusts outsiders."

"Yes, I recall him from my own school days,"

James said. "Always was in trouble with him when he was a principal."

"He didn't much like any of us, did he," Denny added.

"He still doesn't," James said, a dawning expression entering his gaze. "He's been opposing Galen Stallings's building plans at every step. He used some pretty strong language with me when I stood up for Galen's plans at the city council last month. Said I'd be in for a fight if I didn't watch myself."

"Oh, look at the time," Lori said suddenly.

"Yeah, we have to run," Alexis agreed, digging out bills and picking up her ticket.

James stood to let Lori out of the booth and then took the meal ticket from Alexis's hand. "We'll take care of this. Thanks, Lori. Thanks, Teach...."

As Lori hurried toward the front door, Alexis hung back.

"James—" she placed a hand on his arm "—I'd like to explain about yesterday."

"No need, Alexis."

"Yes, there is a need, James." She fingered her umbrella, hoping he hadn't closed her out completely. "But it will have to wait, I guess. I'll call you."

He nodded, but his glance wasn't inviting. Only resigned.

Chapter Seventeen

Alexis sighed for the hundredth time before noon. Some days she may as well give up on accomplishing a lesson in the classroom, she thought. The kids were as restless as jumping beans.

"Let me take them to lunch early," Kathy offered. "If we take a long lunch hour and get some exercise, maybe they'll settle down this afternoon."

"Tyler, please take your seat," Alexis said. The boy tended to wander if she didn't watch him. Early in the year, he'd escaped the classroom twice, and she and Kathy had spent panicky time hunting him.

"Yeah, Tyler. Sit down," Cliff commanded, himself half out of his seat, a combative gleam in his eye. "You're in everybody's way."

"That's enough, Cliff." She gave him a stern look, then turned to Kathy. "Yes, I think a longer lunch hour would help. And it will give me a chance to use the copy machine. Too bad it's raining. Everyone will want to use the gymnasium today.''

Truth to tell, Alexis felt as gloomy as the morning. It seemed to her that whatever she and James had had between them three days ago, now lay in puddles like the rain. With James barely speaking to her, she didn't know how to fix things either. Or when she'd find him alone for any length of time in the near future.

Besides, his mind was wrapped around his crisis, and would be for days and weeks ahead. She felt guilty for even wanting him to think about the two of them.

The day dragged into afternoon and finally to a close with the rain barely diminished to mist. She hurried outside, hoping to intercept James as he picked up Cliff.

Only, it wasn't James there. He had sent Denny.

"Hi, Miss Richmond," Denny said. "I'm here to get Cliff and drop him by Mrs. Shoemaker's place. But can you do me a favor and find Lori for me? I'd like to speak with her a minute."

Alexis swallowed her disappointment and nodded. "Sure."

"Where's my dad?" Cliff asked, staring at Denny with suspicion.

"He had to go over to the county seat," Denny answered, then glanced at Alexis. "Didn't he call to let you know I'd be the one picking him up?"

"Let me check with the office," Alexis said. "Perhaps the call came there."

The office stirred with its usual after-school buzz as

Alexis wove through streaming students to the front desk. She waited for a few moments while the secretary finished a phone call. "Elizabeth, was there a call for me from Mr. Sullivan about his son being picked up by Dennis Bender?"

"Just a minute," Elizabeth said as she shuffled through the stack of messages on the counter. "Um…yeah, guess he did. Sorry it didn't get passed along."

Could her day become any gloomier? James had not called her, he'd called the office. Didn't he trust her any longer? Or was he still…

Could he be angry?

Nothing in his closed demeanor this morning had given her that impression—yet what else was she to think? She had to find out how to get through to him, make him talk to her. What was she going to do if he wouldn't even give them the chance?

"Lori, Denny is outside waiting to drive Cliff to his sitter," she said just as Lori was turning away. "But he wants a word with you."

"Okay. Thanks. Alexis, is everything all right with you?"

"Yeah, sure. I'm fine." Alexis took a deep breath. "But I have to run."

She started back toward her classroom to gather her things, then stopped and pivoted. "Lori!"

Lori, who was almost out of the main door looking out over the parking lot, hesitated. "Yeah?"

"Did you mean what you, uh, implied this morning?" Although none of the kids rushing past her paid her the slightest heed, she felt cautious about her words. "At breakfast?"

"Yes, ma'am, I sure did. Why?"

Alexis nodded. "Just thinking, that's all."

Alexis left school and drove straight home. She made a big pitcher of iced tea, then settled on her couch to make phone calls.

It took her several tries before she found her way past all the voice mail to reach a live response at Galen Stallings's office in Chicago.

"Keith Baldwin speaking. May I help you?"

"Hello, Mr. Baldwin. My name is Alexis Richmond. I'm a teacher in Sunny Creek. I have a matter I'd like to discuss with Mr. Stallings."

"Your name again?"

"Alexis Richmond." She sincerely wished she were part of Sunny Creek's inner circle for a change. Then she wouldn't have to explain every tidbit before achieving her goal. "I need to talk with Mr. Stallings. Is he in?"

"I don't know if he's available, Ms. Richmond. If you'd like to tell me what it concerns…?"

"It concerns a piece of property in Sunny Creek that he may be interested in."

She waited. She sipped her tea and doodled on the legal pad on her coffee table.

"Galen Stallings here." His tone was pleasant, yet he got right to the point. "What is this about?"

She was reminded that no matter how relaxed he may have been in Sullivan's Repair, he was a corporate head. She closed her eyes a moment, hoping she wasn't wasting his time.

"Mr. Stallings, we haven't met properly, but we sort of passed each other in Sullivan's Repair. My name is Alexis Richmond. I'm Cliff Sullivan's teacher."

"Ah, yes. I remember. What can I do for you, Miss Richmond?"

"Well, I'm wondering if you've heard about the big fire in Sunny Creek? It pretty well destroyed the strip mall in which Sullivan's Repair, among other shops, was located."

"Actually, I heard about it this morning, Miss Richmond. From J.D."

"Oh…" The wind went out of her sails. She hadn't figured he'd have talked directly to James. "Oh, then I suppose this call is…unnecessary. I'm sorry to have bothered you."

"Hold on a minute. You called for a reason, didn't you? What was it?"

"Well, I had an idea you might be interested in the property."

"Why would you think that, Miss Richmond?"

"I've really stepped out on a limb here, Mr. Stallings, but if the rumors flying around town are correct, you are more than a bit interested in what is happening in our little town."

"In this case, I'll concede to some truth in rumor. Go on."

In for a penny, in for a pound, she mused.

"Oh, that's good. Well, as you know, this property

is right in the center of the old part of town. Right now it is owned by an absentee landlord who may be interested in selling the land now that it's down to rubble.''

He waited a moment before answering. ''Miss Richmond, why are you telling me all this?''

She bit her lip and swallowed hard. ''I'm sorry if I've interfered in something that is none of my business, Mr. Stallings. I, um— It's only that these shop owners have lost almost everything, and they seem to be getting a bum deal with the current owner. I thought…I merely thought I could find a way to help. I'd hoped you might want to buy the land. I'm sorry if I've mistaken or twisted something I've heard. I'm not usually so rash. Please forgive me. I've acted totally out of line. I'll hang up now.''

''Now hold on there, Miss Richmond. I'm always glad to know what people are saying behind my back—''

She heard amusement in his voice, and wondered what she'd said that was funny.

''And if my plans are to find favor with the long-time residents, it doesn't hurt to invest in the town as it stands now. Does J.D. know you are calling?''

Oh boy. She'd gotten in over her head. Why had she thought this was a good idea?

''No, actually, he doesn't. I—I didn't consult with anyone.''

''Hmm… Now, tell me why I should buy the land?''

''Because it's a good piece of property,'' she said,

stacking her reasons like building blocks. So what if the townspeople would call her a busybody. Stallings could take her suggestions or not, but as long as she'd already made herself look foolish, she might as well forge ahead.

"You can build anything you want to, can't you? The site will take a while to clean up, and I don't think there's anything left of the building to salvage, really. But if you own the land and are willing to pay taxes on it, wouldn't that give you more clout in the local government? You know. Influence with the city council on your plans for the development you hope to build on the edge of town?"

"Yes, I see your line of thinking. Now, why did you favor me with your attention?"

"Why? Well, as I said, I feel sorry for all the shop owners and…and…James Sullivan in particular has made a success of his business."

"And what do you want out of this?"

"I guess…I hoped you might favor James—um, J.D. That perhaps in rebuilding, you might be willing to underwrite a new shop space for him at a reasonable cost."

"I might, at that. Are you sure you haven't spoken with J.D. today?"

"Not since early this morning. I assure you, Mr. Stallings, James doesn't know I'm calling."

"Hmm…I think you should contact him, Miss Richmond. Because you and J.D. have been thinking along the same line. In fact, he's researching the ownership of that property this afternoon. I expect to hear from him before the day is over.''

"Oh?''

"Yes. Only then can we contact the owner and make an offer on the property.''

"Oh.'' Now she did feel stupid. James was way ahead of her. That must be what he was doing over at the county courthouse. What if she'd only made matters between them worse? "I didn't know. Well, thanks for hearing me out, Mr. Stallings.''

"Galen. It sounds as if we might become friends, Miss Richmond. So call me Galen.''

Now what was she to do?

James leaned on the counter in the records department at the county courthouse. He stared at the record, listing the property in Sunny Creek under a strange corporate name: Montgomery Properties. A company name, not an individual, and nowhere did he see the name of Michael Lennox. He'd been making his renter's check out to Michael Lennox for the four years he'd been in the Main Street location.

"Ma'am,'' he asked the clerk, "this doesn't give me all the information I need. When was the property transferred from a single individual to a corporation? How can I find out who that is?''

The clerk gave him several suggestions for finding the information he needed. All the records had been put on computer. Moving into a computer cubicle, he booted up and began his search. He lost track of time as he followed through from one to another, printing out pertinent copies as he went. When he eventually found what he was looking for, his mouth tightened and his eyes narrowed.

He leaned back in his chair and let his hands drop to his lap while his thoughts whirled.

Lori had been right.

The name Wade Fisher topped the list of three people who owned that property and a number of others— all older buildings—in the county. So, Fisher's anxious appearance there the evening of the fire was no accident. He'd been legitimately upset over the fire because his investment was being destroyed.

What had the man hoped to gain by keeping his ownership a secret? He'd collect on his insurance, surely? What was the insurance payout?

J.D. could hardly wait until he brought this information to the other business owners. After all their heretofore fruitless efforts to gain improvements, and their fight against rising rents, they'd have every right to be angry at discovering that their absentee owner was none other than Mr. Wade Fisher. A man who appeared to want the best for Sunny Creek and the county, but who ignored their pleas for building repairs. A man who resisted anything that could raise existing taxes.

Fisher had steadily fought the influence of what he'd called "outsiders." His opposition toward Galen Stallings had been no secret. Now, it seemed to J.D., Fisher's struggle to keep Galen from building his lakeside homes took on a new twist. Taxes, increased land prices, a growing town… What difference did all that make to Fisher? The fact that he would have competition for his properties?

What would happen next as a result of this revelation J.D. didn't know, but he thought Fisher would no longer wield undue influence over the school board or county government. Not when the man's financial secrets were made public. The people James knew took a dim view of such self-centered interest. It smacked of double-dealing.

J.D. called Galen with his information.

"That's very interesting, J.D.," Galen said.

"I suppose this will complicate any effort to buy the property," J.D. said. He tried not to let his discouragement show. "It could take months."

"Yes, it could. But I'm still interested in gaining it. I'll get my people onto it right away. Thanks, James." Then he added, "Have you talked to your teacher friend?"

"My teacher friend? You mean Cliff's teacher?"

"Yes, that's the one. Miss Richmond. You're one lucky man to have so many people in your corner."

"How do you mean?"

"You really don't know?" Galen sounded incredulous. "You two didn't talk about this?"

"About what?" James had a sinking feeling.

"The Main Street property. Approaching me to buy it."

"No," James replied slowly. "We really didn't. We had...other things going on."

"I'll bet." Galen gave a knowing chuckle. "Well, whatever. But she called me an hour ago suggesting

I may be interested in buying it. Gave me quite a sales pitch. If she didn't call me on your behalf—'' he chuckled ''—I'll stand on my head and apologize.''

James drove home in complete puzzlement. Why would Alexis go to all that trouble? He knew she was a compassionate woman and would offer help if she could wherever it was needed. But this—calling Galen?

Did she think James couldn't take care of himself? Was she trying to "fix" him?

Yeah, she liked "fixing" people. She'd been trying to fix him and his son for the past two months. Or maybe she only wanted to mitigate her guilt over dumping him for that pompous-looking yuppy-type guy.

He'd tried to avoid thinking about it, pushing his anger and hurt down while he concentrated on taking care of the hundred and one details he needed to handle after the fire. Now on the long drive home it flooded him.

How could Alexis disregard his feelings so casually? To parade that Ron guy in front of him. After those kisses… He'd begun to think they had a future together.

But to entertain Ron without ever mentioning that she'd changed her mind again. Did that mean she was going to marry the guy? That was what made it so hard—the shock of it.

He was so in love with her it made him nuts, and he'd thought she felt the same. Had that growing passion between them meant so little to her? That honest spiritual connection?

His mouth hardened. There was a fact he had to face. He'd never be anything but a small town man. Why would she want him when he had nothing at all to offer her, not even a healthy income.

No…all spring, it seemed, he'd been living in a dream world. He'd had a growing business, one that he had a talent for. His self-confidence had soared. He had hope for his creative improvements in a popular boat engine. He was making headway with his son. And he'd discovered love.

Well, he still had his son.

And he'd discovered a faith in God, a deep and abiding faith. The kind of faith his mother believed in and kept until her death. He knew that wouldn't change.

As for Alexis…now he had to let her go and return to his reality. Alexis wasn't for him.

Chapter Eighteen

By Thursday afternoon, Alexis knew she was in deeper trouble with James than she'd ever dreamed. Not only had he sent Denny to pick up Cliff each day, but also today he'd sent a note to excuse himself from participating in the field trip tomorrow to the Truman Museum.

Both she and Lori scrambled to find a replacement parent helper. By the end of a lunch hour in which she had no time to eat, she'd talked the sewing mother, Judy, into coming.

After the last bell, she walked slowly home, having left her car home for the day with the vaguest hope that she'd find a ride in a clinky old black truck.

She had to form a plan. She was good at plans. Now she had to have one to cut through the armor James had donned.

He hadn't answered her phone messages.

Notes, sent by Cliff, went unanswered.

Driving by his house showed her no lighted windows and no truck. Where was he spending his nights?

She was loath to discuss her current dilemma with Lori. Lori would just find the whole thing amusing. Phone, notes, drive-bys...

But how could she simply let him go without clearing the air between them? Obviously, he was avoiding her at every turn. And she refused to stoop to questioning Cliff.

That stubborn, hardheaded imbecile! How could James not know she cared about him? *Loved him.* She hadn't meant to hurt his pride.

Stopping cold in her tracks, Alexis stared unseeingly at a bank of brilliant red tulips on the corner of her block. She'd been so smug in her own educational knowledge, in her world of teaching, that she'd done an unforgivable thing. She'd treated James with less respect than she did her students. She was a snob of the worst kind....

Lord, forgive me.... I love him so much....

Two boys whizzed by on bikes. She barely noticed them. Her thoughts spun as she continued to stare blindly at tulip petals and leaves.

Nothing about this situation fit into her usual sense of order. How could she love him so completely after knowing him for only a few weeks? Knowing they had very little in common?

They'd spoken of love several times. God's love. Parental love. A fondness for friends. Never this irresistible attraction that flared between them. They hadn't talked of it, only felt it. Yet what she was experiencing was more than physical attraction. It went far beyond what she'd ever felt for a man before.

She wore no blinders where James was concerned. He had plenty of faults.

So did she! And now she had to face her own snobbery....

He was a bit spoiled where women were concerned. He knew they found him attractive. How many girlfriends had he known over the years?

She'd dated her fair share. She'd always found the men wanting.

None of that mattered—it took nothing away from her love for James.

Sighing, Alexis began to walk again. She mused that James would always be a small-town guy. Someone who had little interest in much beyond his own world. Hardheaded, too. He didn't like authority much. Of any kind, she suspected. A holdover from his own mutinous younger years.

She'd been an obedient child, never rebellious. She'd followed the expected path, seldom stepping out of the picture both she and her parents had painted of her. She'd never failed at anything in her life...*except dating relationships.*

Lord, why can't I find the right balance?

Certainly, she had extended herself when she'd taken a totally unprofessional leap with James. And again when she called Gallen Stallings.

Rightly, James didn't like interference. She had no

clue what he would say when he discovered she'd made that call. Perhaps he already had, and that was deepening his silence. Never mind that her motive had been good, that she had hoped to promote an idea that might benefit James. With James, one had to bring him new ideas but let him feel he was discovering them for himself.

But she *had* overstepped her boundaries in making that call without telling him. She needed to apologize for that. If given a chance…

A plan, a plan…*Lord, please give me direction and wisdom…and a plan.*

School was out next week. Her mom was pressing her to come home for the summer, and her sister Eileen wanted her to travel throughout France and Italy with her. Dad merely said he'd love to see her. She only wished she had a real desire to do either of those things.

Unlocking her door, she threw her things down on the kitchen counter and checked her message machine. Nothing.

Pepper nudged her for attention. "Hi, boy. You are so sweet. Yes, I bet you miss Mom, don't you? And Cliff to play with you?"

She bent and spent a long time petting him, then took him for a quick walk. Returning, she fed him, vowing to take him home on Saturday.

Her tummy growled, reminding her she'd missed lunch. She pulled out a bag of precut salad and poured some into a bowl. She nibbled, wondering where

James was at this moment. At the site, still cleaning away rubble?

Maybe she'd drive by on her way to Bible Study.

She had to find him.

There were a few curious people staring at the ugly torn walls, but only one man patrolling the area against unwanted invaders. She didn't see a black truck as she drove by.

She wanted to scream with disappointment. James wasn't there, nor was Denny. There were only a couple of people from the other shops.

She packed away her dashed hopes and turned her little car down the street that held her church. Bible Study was beginning a new topic tonight. Maybe she'd find solace in the scriptures.

The old black truck sat in the parking lot. James...

Her heart began to race. She parked next to it and slid out of her seat with a spring. After the heavy week he'd had, Alexis hadn't dreamed James would push himself to attend.

She reached the classroom their group used, and paused in the doorway. Her gaze flew to James's tall slouched figure, one ankle crossed on a knee. His Bible lay ready, his long fingers spread against it, holding it loosely. Denny sat next to him.

"Hi, everyone," she murmured softly. James nodded. An acknowledgment of her presence, nothing more.

"There you are, dear," Caroline said. "We've been waiting for you. Now we can start."

Alexis found a chair opposite James. Fitz opened with prayer and then began the study. Every bit as strongly as she had the first time he'd come, Alexis found his presence distracting. Was he as aware of her? Several times she felt his warm gaze. But by the time she turned his way, he was looking elsewhere.

After the closing prayer, she lingered. She talked to Caroline and the others as they all strolled outside together. As long as James stayed in sight, she tarried.

"Man, I'm beat," Denny said. He headed toward his red truck. "I'm heading home for some sleep."

"Me, too," James said. "Gotta pick up Cliff from Mrs. Shoemaker's, then I'm for home."

From the corner of her eye, she saw him open his truck door. Alexis broke off her conversation. "James?"

"Um, hi, Alexis," he rushed to say. He got into his seat and closed his door. Then he hung out the window. "Sorry I can't do the field trip tomorrow. But Cliff is looking forward to it."

"Yes, all the kids are," she said slowly. Then, no longer caring who heard her, she asked, "James, can I talk to you?"

"Honest, Alexis. The day just wasn't working out for me."

"It's not that," she snapped. He was being deliberately dense.

"Well, if Cliff's behavior is causing more problems, I won't object to another detention. It won't hurt him. As you've said, he has to learn the consequences of his actions."

She gritted her teeth. How far was he going to carry this?

"I wasn't exactly thinking of Cliff, James. I—

There's more to talk about than…'' Couldn't he see
how much she wanted to get this misunderstanding
between them straightened out? "I'd like to talk about
what's going on with you.''

"Got my hands full with getting my business put
back together," he said tersely. "That's what's going
on with me. You should know that.''

"Yes, I do know. That's not all, though. There's—''

He turned his key, starting his motor. It roared as
he pumped the gas pedal.

"It's all I can handle for now. I've no time for
anything else. Thanks for all your help with my kid,
Teach. You'll gain brownie points with all the extra
effort you put out. Gotta go now. Promised Cliff I'd
be there on time. See you around.''

All the extra effort she put out?

He peeled off, leaving her staring after him, her
heart shrinking to a tiny crumpled ball.

James sat on a tall stool in the single, detached ga-
rage at the rear of his rental house. He'd set up a
temporary shop here. He could no longer go without
some income.

He'd been lucky. After spending days taking an inventory for the insurance company, he'd been allowed
to recover a few of his tools. His credit card had paid
for replacements until his insurance kicked in. He'd
put a sign out on the fire site, directing his customers
here. Many of his customers had sought him out.

Thank God for the work. At least for him, starting

from square one again wasn't the worst thing that could happen. Getting down to it, working with his hands, was what he did best.

The door lay open to the streaming May sunshine. He carefully dipped a rag into cleaning solvent, then tackled the task of cleaning a boat motor. Repairing things, an honest service that he could offer and that people needed—it gave him satisfaction to know he could do well at something.

He concentrated on the task in front of him. Cliff skateboarded in front of the house. James liked that, too. Knowing his son was close by on a sunny Saturday where he could keep track of him.

He refused to think about Alexis. Too painful. He must've been temporarily out of his mind!

But no more. Now he had his feet on the ground.

If only his heart didn't yank like a hooked fish when he glimpsed a honey-haired woman on the street. Or jerk him out of a deep sleep, listening for her soft murmuring voice. On Thursday night, he'd gritted his teeth against the yearning that threatened to overwhelm him. He'd barely made it through the sweet appeal in the parking lot without grabbing her like a starving kid, and embarrassing her by kissing her there in front of everyone.

But no more. That was over.

A familiar late-model Jeep parked at the curb. James heard the door slam and glanced up.

"Hi, Galen." James wiped his hands on an old towel and strode forward to meet his best customer. "I see you found me."

"Wasn't hard, J.D. The town's not that big and you have lots of friends."

"So I do." He realized it was true. "They've been loyal. I only hope the other shop owners are finding as much support as I've been given. Have you found out anything more about the property?"

"That's what I came by to tell you. Time will tell, but I don't think it will be hard to purchase. And I tend to think your Mr. Fisher is out of the public servant business. He's under investigation by the powers-that-be for conflict of interest."

James nodded. "That's good. I know a number of people who will be happy to hear it." Alexis wouldn't have to swallow that slippery hound's snide insults any longer.

"Say, I called the company about your new life vests," James said, changing the subject, "and they said your order is en route. I've taken care of redirecting my shipping address, so they should come along in a day or two. Can I offer you a cola or ice water?"

"Sure, I could use a long drink of cold water."

James stepped to his picnic cooler and hauled out a jug of water. He filled a large paper cup to the rim.

"How long are you expecting to do business here?" Galen asked.

"As long as it takes to rebuild my customer base," James answered. "I'm looking at renting another shop space, but anything with a good location is worth a king's ransom."

Galen leaned his shoulder against the wall. "Seems that way all over. I'd as soon own my own buildings."

"Sure. Sure. If I had the money…"

"Can't you borrow it?"

"Could, I suppose. But I'm not too sure I could get a loan. My credit has been…a bit unsteady."

"What about a private loan?"

James laughed outright, and when he spoke his wry tone was apparent. "I have friends in town, Galen, but lots of these people have long memories, too. They still think of me as the rebellious kid roaring around town in a souped-up truck, raising a good bit of cane. I'd have better luck selling my design improvement for the current four-stroke engine."

"Have you patented it? Would you be willing to show me that design?"

James stared at the older man for a moment. "Sure, I guess so. I filled out a patent application a month ago. It's not in your field, though."

"Maybe you're not aware of all my companies, J.D. I have a couple of manufacturing plants, and I make as well as sell hospital equipment. I've been looking into broadening my product output. Tooling up to make a boat engine wouldn't be beyond my capabilities if I believed your design a good one."

"You'd be willing to buy it?"

"Let's see what you've got."

Chapter Nineteen

"You can earn prizes," Alexis explained to her twelve students. It was the last day of school, and she and Kathy passed out red folders with charts and packets of silver and gold star stickers. "Keep up your reading throughout the summer. Every time you read a book, have your mom or dad put a star on your chart and their initials."

Heather raised her hand. "How many books do we have to read?"

"That's up to you, Heather," Alexis replied. This was a plan she and Kathy had had approved only in the past week. Alexis had no great hope of a big success with the program, but anything would be a plus. She had quietly put funds into a special bank account to cover the cost. The way she figured it, whatever it cost was a small price to pay for her students gaining a little ground. She continued to explain. "The more books you read, the bigger the prize. You can win a gift certificate from your favorite hamburger place or you can earn points that turn into spending dollars at the video store.''

"And there are lots of books to choose from at Sunny Creek's library,'' Kathy added. "The librarians there already know of our program, so you can talk to Mrs. McKnight. She'll help you.''

"When do we get our prizes?'' Tyler asked.

"Bring your charts into the office during the first week in September and you'll get the prize you've earned,'' Alexis said.

"What if we don't want to read?'' Kevin complained. Kevin was the slowest reader student Alexis taught, and she'd racked her brain all year to motivate him.

"You don't have to, dunce,'' Tyler said. "But I'm gonna do it. I'm gonna earn all the prizes.''

"No, you're not,'' Cliff said on a snort. "I can read better than you.''

"That's enough, you two.'' For a change, their competition made Alexis want to laugh. Just maybe it would spark both of them to read a little more than required. "I'd hate to give you detention on the last day of school.''

Cliff sat straighter and made a zipping motion against his mouth.

Alexis glanced at her watch. "Okay, everyone, gather up all your things and line up by the door.''

She and Kathy waited while the scramble erupted, then settled into a line at the door. Heather lagged, her blue eyes misting. She broke from the line and rushed to hug Alexis. "I'll miss you, Miss Richmond."

"I'll miss you, too, Heather," Alexis replied, returning the child's hug. She leaned closer. "But I'm very proud of the progress you've made this year."

"Me, too," Kathy said, as another student followed Heather's example, hugging Kathy and then Alexis.

Hiding her own tugging emotions, Alexis picked up a bag of giant suckers and passed them out as a parting gift.

"I'll miss you all. But I'll be here next year, and some of you are coming back into my room. Now, have a good summer." The bell rang, right on the dot at noon. "You are excused."

"Are you all set?" Kathy asked as the noise began to decrease.

"Yes." Alexis gazed around the room. It always looked bare and lonely at the close of a year. "As soon as I gather up the turtle and goldfish. The tank will have to stay—it's too big for me to carry. I can't believe I overlooked finding someone to take care of them for the summer. Now I'll have to find a small fishbowl. Or two."

"Well, I would, but I'll have my hands full with my daughter's pregnancy. It's been great serving with you this year, Alexis. I've learned a lot by being a part of your team."

"I appreciate all your hard work, too, Kathy." Alexis pulled out a small gift, a sterling silver charm bracelet that she'd chosen for her assistant, and handed it to her. ''I couldn't have gotten along without you. Seriously.''

Alexis spent the afternoon packing up for the summer. Even assured she'd return the following season, she had things to clear out. By three, she had everything, she thought, and made one last trip from the classroom to her car with the fish in a large plastic bag and the turtle in a shoe box.

She set the box on the floor on the passenger side. As she started her car, she stared down at the turtle, his neck stretched out to investigate the cardboard box. Dare she ask Cliff to care for these little creatures?

Why not?

What he really needed was a puppy. She'd never gotten around to suggesting that to James.

Who was she kidding? What she really wanted was an excuse to see James.

Alexis hadn't seen James since last week. On Saturday she'd gone to her parents' house to return Pepper. She'd delayed returning to Sunny Creek until dusk on Sunday evening. She'd missed both morning and evening worship services. Missed mingling with her local friends. Missed James...

It wouldn't hurt to run by his house and just *ask*. Cliff might actually want the critters.

Though she drove slowly, she covered the few blocks in five minutes.

A knot of preschool children played in the yard next door, watched by a young mother sitting on her front steps. Cliff was nowhere in sight and neither was

James, but she caught a radio playing a country music tune from somewhere in the rear of his house.

She tucked a loose lock of hair behind her ear, sucked in a deep breath for courage and got out of the car. She reached for the turtle box and the sealed plastic bag with the three goldfish darting about. They couldn't remain in there for long, she was sure. She followed the sound of a twangy guitar.

James knelt on the concrete floor, his back curled around one upraised knee, his other leg beneath him. It appeared he was putting together steel shelves. The old white T-shirt stretched tight over his shoulders. The sleeves rolled to the shoulder exposed his long muscled arms. He reached for a tool, his hands exhibiting strength in motion, getting the screw into place.

He was doing what he did best. Making something, repairing something.

She moistened her dry lips. "Hi, James."

His head shot up, his gaze locking with hers. For a moment, she caught a flash of pure joy shining from his brown eyes at the sight of her. It sent a soaring hope straight to her heart. He was glad to see her.

Then, just as quickly, his expression became guarded.

"Hi, Alexis." He returned his attention to his task. "I'm surprised you're still in town."

"I live here," she quipped, refusing to let his cynical tone upset her. He *was* happy to see her. She felt like whooping for joy. His feelings for her hadn't really changed, they'd only gone underground. He felt the same as before. "I have things to do here. Where's Cliff?"

"At the pool with Robby and his mom." He gave her a lopsided smile, which set her heart bouncing. "Sara has agreed to help with Cliff over the summer and they're going to camp out this weekend. The boys are celebrating being out of school."

"Yeah, me, too. Um, I mean I intend to as soon as I wrap up a few final details. I thought maybe Cliff would look after our classroom goldfish and turtle for the summer."

"He'd probably like that. Come July, I'm going to get him a puppy for his birthday."

"That's a great idea," she said, pleased that James had been attuned to his son without her prompting. "He was so good with Pepper."

"He was, at that."

"Then, can I leave these with you?" She held up the sealed plastic bag of fish. "I'll have to find a fish-bowl or something for them. The tank at school stays there."

"Never mind, Alexis." He rose, reaching for the always handy towel to wipe his hands before accepting the fish and turtle. "I think I have something that will do."

"Thanks. I do appreciate it... How are the other shop owners doing?"

"About like you'd expect. The Carpet Corner has already found another location." He spoke as if answering on rote, his tone going into neutral. "I think Bea from the flea market is retiring altogether. The bookshop owner doesn't know yet what she will do. As far as I know, all the insurances have come through.''

''Ah… Well, at least they have that.'' She looked about her at the way he'd organized the small space. ''Do you plan to stay here?''

''Only as long as necessary. I have something in the works, but I can't talk about it yet. Too soon.'' All at once he hung his thumbs from his back pockets, straightening his shoulders, and looked at her directly. ''Listen, Alexis. I want to thank you for all the attention you've given my boy this spring. You're a teacher among teachers. I'll— We'll always be grateful.''

He was saying goodbye? *No…he can't. Not until he knows I love him. Lord, is this Your plan?*

She swallowed hard, fighting the sudden tears that threatened to spill. It seemed he'd made a decision without hearing her out.

''I've been happy to teach Cliff. We…you…um…''

She turned away swiftly, before she could make a total fool of herself. ''I guess I'd better run along. I— I have things to do.''

Alexis blinked awake the following morning. Near her bedroom window, a bird chirped in the first gray light of morning. She hadn't slept well, tossing until almost two a.m. Yet that wasn't what had waken her.

At her door, someone tapped insistently. *Who…?*

James! The only person she knew who would wake her at this hour.

She shot out of bed, grabbing her print summer robe as she stumbled through the apartment toward the door.

She snapped on the outside light and opened her door as far as the chain would allow. "James?"

"Yeah, it's me. Get dressed, okay?"

She brushed her hair out of her eyes. "What for? Are we going fishing again?"

"Just get dressed. In jeans, your oldest sneakers and a warm top layer."

"You're not going to tell me?"

"You've got five minutes."

"It isn't an emergency, is it? No one is hurt or anything?"

He made a point of checking his watch. "Four and a half minutes. I'll wait right here."

"You're serious, huh?"

He raised a brow.

"All right, all right." She slammed the door closed. Racing back to her bedroom, she dressed in record time.

"What is this all about?" she asked a few minutes later when she rejoined him.

He took her arm and carefully steered her down the stairs. "I'm not sure. We're going to find out."

"*You're* not sure?"

"Not about much." He opened the truck door, his hand wrapping around her elbow to help her up.

In long purposeful strides he circled the truck and climbed in. He settled into his seat, then thoughtfully stared at her for a moment.

"There's food in the bag," he said, nodding to the brown paper bag at her feet. He turned on the motor, put the truck in gear and pulled away from the curb. "Coffee in the thermos."

"Are you hungry?" she asked, pulling out sausage-and-egg sandwiches.

"Starved."

He drove out of town and turned down the same side road he had used once before. "Aren't your friends down yet?"

"Yeah, they've been down. I called Galen to let him know I'd be taking the boat out."

Alexis didn't respond, and James remained quiet for the remainder of the drive. When they reached the clearing, he parked close to the boat dock. She saw no one, although two vehicles sat in front of the huge cabin, evidence that someone was home.

Sunlight already warmed the air. She took a deep appreciative breath of it, loving the dawn's quiet promise. With James's assistance, she stepped into the boat and smiled at him. "Are you sure you trust me not to ruin your fishing?"

His mouth curled, and his gaze was teasing. "Not this time."

He started the motor, carefully steering the boat out of the dock area before increasing speed. Alexis found a cushion and leaned against the seat in back. Alexis had forgotten to bring a hat. She closed her eyes and raised her face to the sun.

After a few moments, James throttled back, bringing the boat into the same quiet cove they'd visited before. He anchored, then turned and stretched his legs in front of him.

The trees were in full leaf now, and the surrounding land looked dense and a bit mysterious. For the first time, Alexis realized he didn't have his fishing rods with him. "Don't you plan to fish?"

"Not this morning. I want to talk, and this place is..." He glanced around them. "Peaceful. Like it's one of God's special places. I feel closer to Him when I'm here."

"Yes, it's a lovely spot," she murmured, her heart unfurling in wonder. She'd asked God for a plan... "What do you want to talk about?"

"Us."

"Is there an us?" She held her breath.

"Hope so. After that look in your eyes yesterday... It tore me up, Alexis. I wanted to..." He pursed his lips, his chin thrusting forward. He glanced away, as though he dared not look at her. "Made me wonder. Couldn't sleep, and when I finally dozed, I woke with this wild urge to see you."

His gaze swung back to her, an agony of hurt and uncertainty there. "But I have to know, Alexis. Tell me straight to my face. What about that city guy? Are you going to marry him? Ol' what's-his-name?"

"His name is Ron. No," she said, enunciating her words with quiet distinction. "I'm not going to marry him."

"Why not? You were engaged, weren't you?"

"Almost. Not quite." She chewed on the inside of her lip a moment, thinking about the truth she'd only recently discovered. "You see, even though we talked of marrying, he never gave me a ring or really followed through with any plans that included me. So the engagement was really only *my* dream. Then I, um, discovered something very silly about myself, James. I found out that I was looking for the wrong dream."

"You were? What's the right dream?"

"You—if you want me, James."

"Want you? Do you even have to *ask?*" He shoved a hand restlessly through his hair. His smile flashed, still uncertain, but filled with joy. "If you only knew how many nights thinking about you has kept me awake. I…if I…But why do you want me? I flunked out before as a husband. As a father, too, but I'm changing that. And I have so little to give you."

She reached for his hand, folding her fingers into his. "Listen here, James. You have more to give in your little finger than many men have in their entire body. You have that deep-seated integrity that comes along very rarely, I think."

As she spoke, his gaze grew softer. As soft and sweet as brown sugar.

"You work hard to make a living," she continued. "There's not a lazy bone in you. And underneath your overrated rebellious streak lies the most honest, generous heart I've ever known. That's enough to fill a whole lifetime. I just hope…"

Carefully, he came forward and kneeled, sliding his arms around her waist. He bent his forehead against hers, gently rocking back and forth, touching her nose with his.

"What?" he breathed. "What is it you hope, Alexis?"

Her throat was so clogged with emotion that she could hardly speak. "I pray you want to spend that lifetime with me."

"Is this a proposal of marriage?" His voice uneven, he touched his mouth to hers once, twice, while warmth radiated between them. When he finally drew away they merely stared at each other for a long moment.

"Yes," she finally muttered. "Yes it is. I want exclusive rights to all your kisses."

He grabbed her hand and clasped it tightly in his own. As though he'd never let it go. "In that case, Alexis…I pledge them to you for a lifetime. At least a hundred years to come. I love you."

"I love you, too," she whispered.

His mouth came down on hers once more with gentle promise. Then he raised his head and his smile held a hyped, boyish gleam. "Now let's get back. I have something to show you."

"What is it?"

"You'll see, Alexis…. You'll see."

Her heart beating with joy, Alexis could hardly wait to see what he had in store for her.

Epilogue

The old Bender farm was already teeming with Labor Day picnic activity by the time James, Alexis, Cliff and Robby arrived. James parked the truck in line with three other cars. Following their lead, Lori and Steven parked their car next to the truck. The boys were off and running as soon as their feet hit the ground.

"I'll see they stay out of trouble," Tina said.

"Don't go just yet," Alexis said.

"Hi, you two." Caroline came forward to greet them warmly. "And Lori and Steven. Welcome. We've been waiting for you."

"Sorry we're late, Caroline," Alexis said. "We brought Lori and Steven along with us, and then James wanted to run by the construction site to check on things this morning."

"I hear it's going to be one fancy set of shops," Fitz remarked, unfolding more lawn chairs under the big spreading oak tree. "When will it be finished?"

"Coming right along, Fitz," James answered. "Galen doesn't believe in doing anything halfway."

"I've heard that about the man," Fitz said with a nod.

"Y' know, he's taken my advice about how to lay out the new Sullivan's Small Motors and Repair. What's even nicer is that I own a piece of it. I feel kinda bad about taking the lion's share of the new shop space, but not all of the shop owners wanted to come back to our location anyway, so I think it's all working out. And by the looks of it, I think we'll make our Thanksgiving Day opening just fine."

"That should be really something," Lori interjected.

"That all sounds so exciting." Caroline turned to Alexis and Lori. "And how is the new school year shaping up? Are you happy with it?"

"Sure am," Alexis replied. "I have only ten students this year, and my para, Kathy, is a dream to have. But the air-conditioning isn't working very well and we're all stifling in this heat. Makes the kids even more restless than usual."

"Always something, right?" Caroline said.

"Seems that way," Alexis murmured, her eyes dreamy. She smiled and fluttered her left hand in the air. "But I do have something new to show you."

"Alexis," Lori squeaked, and grabbed Alexis's hand to study the sparkling engagement ring that adorned her third finger. "You didn't say a word."

"We're announcing it now," Alexis said on a chuckle. "Cliff is happy with our decision, too. He thinks it will be easier on him when we are living together and not running back and forth between houses. And it will be.''

The busy summer had sped by. At the last minute, she'd signed on to sub for summer classes. It gave her employment while James worked to create the new shop. Now she and James squeezed in every possible moment of time for themselves.

James slipped an arm around her waist, his eyes twinkling. ''Yes, we want you all to know how much we appreciate your support this year. You've been terrific friends. I couldn't have handled everything nearly so well without you, the Lord and Alexis.''

Congratulations, back pats, and hugs reigned on them from the group.

After a few moments, Lori asked the inevitable question. ''When?''

''Christmas Eve,'' Alexis said. ''That way we can start a new year married.''

''Sounds dreamy to me,'' Tina said.

''Me, too,'' chimed Lori.

Alexis simply smiled. Real life with James—and Cliff—would be so much better than any dream.

*   *   *   *   *

Dear Reader,

A society is often judged by how it treats those in its society that are nonstandard. The growing awareness and treatment of students with Behavior Disorder is a case in point. These students sometimes have physical disabilities, sometimes emotional, but all deserve a chance to learn and shine in their knowledge. This story touches that need. God loves each of us with a passion beyond description.

I hope you enjoy Alexis and James's story. They are typical of all the small-town folks who live around the lakes. Just like you and me.

You may write to me at: P.O. Box 1221, Blue Springs, MO 64015.

Ruth Scofield

THE PREACHER'S DAUGHTER

BY

LYN COTE

Growing up, Lucie Hansen had resented
the restrictions placed on her as a "preacher's kid."
So would the preacher's daughter realize she'd make
the perfect pastor's wife for Tanner Bond, the
handsome minister who needed her help in
uniting his new community?

Don't miss
THE PREACHER'S DAUGHTER
On sale September 2003

Available at your favorite retail outlet.

SAMANTHA'S GIFT

BY
VALERIE HANSEN

The local teacher was showing Sean Bates around
town and the gossips were working overtime,
creating a romance between the new guidance
counselor and teacher Rachel Woodward. But when
little Samantha entered their lives, Rachel knew
Sean would make a perfect father…and husband,
leaving her wondering if God would have a place
for Rachel in this budding family.

Don't miss
SAMANTHA'S GIFT
On sale August 2003.

Available at your favorite retail outlet.

A LOVE BEYOND

BY

KATE WELSH

Jim Lovell was hiding something…and Crystal Alton
knew it. His rugged charm couldn't hide the fact that
her inquisitive new ranch hand could barely ride a
horse. But would the secret he kept—that he was a
detective on assignment—keep Jim from the paradise
God had shown him with Crystal?

Don't miss

A LOVE BEYOND
On sale August 2003.

Available at your favorite retail outlet.

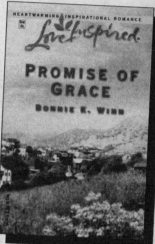

PROMISE OF GRACE

BY

BONNIE K. WINN

The only miracle in jilted and injured
Grace Stanton's life was Dr. Noah Brady.
The small-town Texas surgeon could treat her
wounds, but could his healing touch mend her
broken heart and restore her shattered faith?

Don't miss

PROMISE OF GRACE

On sale September 2003

Available at your favorite retail outlet.

LIP•